AND HUBBY MAKES THREE

A TRAGICALLY *FABULOUS* LOVE STORY

AND HUBBY MAKES THREE

A TRAGICALLY *FABULOUS* LOVE STORY

MICHAEL McHALE

HENNESSEY HOUSE PUBICATIONS

And Hubby Makes Three
A Tragically *Fabulous* Love Story

Copyright 2024 Michael McHale

Hennessey House Publications

HennesseyHousePublications@gmail.com

Michael McHale

MichaelMcHaleAuthor@gmail.com

Cover design: MSM Designs
Cover and back cover photos: Robert Cooper Burlingham
About the Author photo: Bart Mastronardi
headshotsbybart.com
Cover Models: Michael McHale, Melinda Chilton, Colin Lawrence

DEDICATION

This book is dedicated to every LGBTQIA+ community member and those who love them.

This book is also dedicated to the most amazing individual I have ever met in my life, my partner in life, my husband Bob Burlingham, who has *never* let me give up on my dreams no matter how ridiculous they may seem to have been at the time. Thank you Bob.
I love you.

6

TABLE OF CONTENTS

8

INTRODUCTION

This book was originally written as a feature film script back in 1997 with the same title, so any references to marriage not being legal yet for the LGBTQIA+ Community is due to that fact.

I had considered 'updating' it when I adapted my script into this book but I decided to keep it in it's purest form, a time when the LGBTQIA+ Community did not have the legal right to marry who they truly loved with all of their heart.

I do not want the Community and it's allies to ever forget the struggle and the fight that so many of us endured for such a long and heartbreaking time before same-sex marriage became legal in the United States back on that glorious Friday, June 26, 2015.

I never take for granted the rights that have been afforded to me as a gay man and am grateful every day for my amazing husband Bob who captured my heart back on Saturday, October 11, 2003.

On a lighter note. I came up with the idea for this story when my dear friend Jordan Monks and myself were having conversations about how lucky she was to be able to get married at the time and I shared with her my own dreams of having a fairy tale wedding. We joked about having a fun wedding just so I could have that experience.

After days of pondering this, Wendy and Mitch were born and I wrote the original first draft of the feature film in three days which is still available to make into a movie… hopefully with Jonathan Bailey (from Bridgerton & WICKED) as Mitch…hint hint.

Finally, I would be remiss if I did not mention that, as an author, Armistead Maupin has had the greatest influence on me and that's one of the reasons this story is set in San Francisco, besides the fact that it is also one of my favorite cities. His books *Tales of the City* is by far one of the greatest series of all time and I have devoured each book dozens of times over the years.

So it is my hope that you will feel a vibe from that beautiful series throughout my book. I am grateful to my friend Maren Knight who presented me with the first Tales of the City on my 25th birthday many (many) years ago. That's where the seeds of inspiration were planted. If you have not read his series, go…read them now…you will thank me later.

Chapter One: The Perfect Pair

Some friendships were written in the stars. Others, like Wendy Chilton and Mitch Pratt's, were written in spilled coffee and ugly tears in a college cafeteria. Ten years ago, Wendy had been crying over her latest breakup when she'd accidentally dumped her latte all over Mitch's freshly dry-cleaned Ralph Lauren sweater. Instead of getting angry, he simply said, "Honey, if he's not worth your MAC waterproof mascara, he's not worth your tears." They have been inseparable ever since.

Now, on a perfectly breezy San Francisco afternoon, they were doing what they did best: making something simple into an absolute spectacle. Their rainbow kite swooped and dove among dozens of others dotting the sky above Golden Gate Park, their laughter carrying on the wind as they struggled to keep it airborne.

"Left! No, your other left!" Wendy shouted, her strawberry-blonde hair whipping around her face as she bounced on her toes. "Mitch, seriously, how are you this bad at this?"

"I'm sorry, did you want to take over?" Mitch's designer sunglasses slipped down his nose as he concentrated. "Because I'm pretty sure the last time you tried, we nearly decapitated that poor jogger."

"That was not my fault! The wind changed direction!"

"The wind changed direction," Mitch mimicked in a falsetto that sounded nothing like her. "You keep telling yourself that sweetie."

Their moment of perfect flight ended in spectacular fashion as their kite tangled with four others, creating an aerial traffic jam that sent all five kites plummeting toward earth. Wendy collapsed onto the grass, clutching her sides with laughter.

"Have you ever had a problem keeping it up before?" she managed between giggles.

Mitch shot her a look that could have wilted flowers. "Oh, so *I'm* the problem here?"

Their laughter mingled together as Wendy reached up and smacked his butt playfully. It was the kind of easy, physical affection they'd always shared, the kind that made people do double-takes and ask if they were a couple. The answer always made them laugh harder: "Yes, but with different men."

Later, sprawled on a checkered blanket with the remains of their picnic lunch scattered between them, Wendy watched Mitch's face anxiously as he chewed. She'd spent three hours on this chicken casserole, following her mother's recipe to the letter. But judging by the way Mitch's jaw was working overtime, she might as well have served him cardboard.

"Well?" she sweetly prompted. "What do you think?"

Mitch, who could never tell a lie to save his life (a quality that had gotten him into more than one scrape at his job designing window displays for Nordstrom), tried to maintain his diplomatic expression. It was a losing battle with his mouth full of her latest culinary experiment. He swallowed with visible effort.

"Let's just say I hope the magic of marriage includes the ability to cook."

"Hey!" But Wendy was laughing more than protesting. After all, this was the man who'd once ordered pizza to her apartment at midnight because he couldn't bear the thought of her eating the "sad excuse for stir-fry" she'd made.

"You want me to be honest, don't you?" Mitch's eyes sparkled with mischief as he took another tiny bite, his dramatic grimace worthy of a soap opera.

Wendy nodded, pulling her knees up to her chest. "I guess I just want to be the perfect wife. And that should include being able to boil water."

Mitch abandoned his plate and wrapped an arm around her shoulders, pulling her close. His cologne - the expensive kind he insisted was worth every penny - wrapped around her like a familiar hug. "Look Wendy, you already are the perfect wife, just not married yet. What's the big deal with eating out anyway? Lots of couples do it!"

"I know, but I don't want to be like other couples, ya know?" She leaned into his embrace, grateful not for the first time that she had a best friend who understood her better than she understood herself sometimes. Mitch had been there through everything - terrible dates, worse breakups, and finally meeting Bruce, the man who'd changed her mind about happy endings.

"I just don't want you to change for the marriage. You're wonderful just the way you are." He tossed his chicken back into the casserole dish with an unceremonious plop. "So... cooking isn't your strong suit. Big deal! There are other qualities you excel in. Focus on those, okay?"

Wendy followed his lead, dumping her own barely touched portion back. "Maybe I'll just stick with floral arrangements."

"There you go! That's the spirit!" Mitch jumped to his feet, pulling her up with him. His blue eyes sparkled with an idea - always a dangerous sign. "You want something at the snack shack?"

"Oh God yes!" Wendy linked her arm through his as they headed across the grass, the late afternoon sun painting everything golden. "I mean," she mimicked his earlier diplomatic tone, "that would be nice."

As they walked, Wendy couldn't help but smile. In seven days, she would be Mrs. Bruce Hollingsworth, starting a whole new chapter of her life. But some things would never change - like the fact that her best friend would always be there to tell her the truth about her cooking, support her dreams, and lead her toward better food options. Even if those options involved hot dogs from a park snack stand.

Behind them, a seagull descended on their abandoned picnic blanket, took one bite of the chicken casserole, spit it out and promptly flew away. Some things, Wendy thought, watching it go, were better left to the professionals.

Chapter Two: Games of Chance

The carnival lights twinkled against the darkening San Francisco sky, turning the night into a kaleidoscope of color and movement. Wendy and Mitch shared a cloud of cotton candy between them as they strolled past the rides, their shoulders bumping companionably. The sugar dissolved on Wendy's tongue, sweet and familiar, just like these moments with her best friend.

They stopped at one of those deceptively simple carnival games - six milk jugs stacked in a pyramid, looking as innocent as they were impossible to knock down. Mitch handed over a five-dollar bill with the kind of misplaced confidence that had once led him to believe he could cut his own hair (a disaster that Wendy had documented extensively for posterity).

"Watch this," he whispered to her. "I'm going to win you something spectacular."

His first throw went so wide it nearly hit a passing cotton candy vendor, who shot him a look that suggested this wasn't the first time he'd had to dodge projectiles tonight.

"I was just getting warmed up," Mitch assured her, his cheeks flushing pink beneath the carnival lights.

"Whatever you say, Mitch." Wendy bit back a smile, remembering similar claims from their college softball team's charity game, where Mitch had somehow managed to hit himself with his own bat.

The second ball was even worse than the first, causing the carnival worker to duck behind his counter with the practiced ease of someone who'd seen it all before.

"Hey! Are these things magnetized or what?" Mitch's indignation would have been more convincing if his last throw hadn't gone in the complete opposite direction of the target.

The man behind the booth handed him his final ball with a world-weary sigh. "Maybe it's ya throwing."

Wendy's laugh earned her a glare from Mitch before he wound up for his final attempt. The ball went sailing past the booth entirely, narrowly missing a man whose toupee went flying in surprise. The carnival worker, clearly deciding that customer safety trumped game integrity, thrust a tiny stuffed dog at Mitch.

"Here! Here!" he practically begged. "Take it! You won, okay? Just... please stop throwing things!"

Mitch accepted his consolation prize with as much dignity as he could muster, presenting it to Wendy with an elaborate bow. "Your booty, m'love!"

"God, Mitch, you call that a throw!"

He snatched the dog back, pressing it to his chest in mock offense. "Oh, and I suppose you could do better!"

"Blindfolded, in another state!"

They returned to the booth, where the worker visibly flinched at their approach. Wendy stepped up, her competitive spirit - the same one that had made her undefeated champion of their Thursday night bar trivia team - burning bright.

"Don't worry," she assured the worried worker. "This time it's for me." She turned to Mitch with a smirk. "Remember, at least you can cook."

Her first throw barely missed, causing Mitch to crow with delight. "Hey! What about the blindfold? All that big talk..."

"Fine!"

She pulled a silk scarf from her purse - the same one she'd used to blindfold Mitch during his surprise birthday party last month. The carnival worker instinctively protected his hairpiece as she tied it around her eyes. The crowd that had gathered held their breath as she wound up and threw.

The crash of milk jugs hitting the ground was almost as satisfying as Mitch's shocked expression. Wendy whipped off the blindfold and let out a victory whoop that would have made her high school softball coach proud.

"Hey! You were supposed to be in another state," Mitch declared as they walked away, Wendy's arms full of the enormous stuffed animal she'd won.

Their laughter carried across the carnival grounds as they made their way through the crowd, sharing a blue raspberry Slurpee and adding to Wendy's growing collection of prizes. The night air was cool against their skin, carrying the mingled scents of popcorn, cotton candy, and possibility.

"So," Mitch ventured after a while, his tone trying for casual and missing by a mile, "are you nervous?"

Wendy shrugged, but he knew her well enough to see past the attempted nonchalance. "A little, I guess."

"A little?! I'm a wreck!"

She tapped him playfully on the shoulder. "And you don't even have to walk down the aisle!"

"Yeah! What's up with that anyway? Why is it that the bride gets to walk down the aisle? Never the groom."

"Hmm." Wendy pretended to consider it deeply. "Cause men are too lazy?"

"Hey! I resent that!"

"Oh, come on! When was the last time you actually changed a channel without using a remote?"

"Uh, TiVo, DVD, or CD player?"

"See my point?"

"Touché."

They ended the night at Le Petit Jardin, their favorite restaurant in North Beach, where the maître d' had long since stopped asking if they wanted separate tables. As they swayed together on the tiny dance floor, Wendy felt the familiar comfort of Mitch's embrace, the same one that had held her through breakups, celebrations, and everything in between.

"You know," Mitch murmured, "in seven days you'll be doing this with your Dad, and then I'll really be jealous!"

She giggled and snuggled closer into his chest, breathing in the familiar scent of his cologne. "You know what?"

"What?"

"I love having you as my best friend. It makes getting married so much easier, you know?"

Mitch nodded as they continued to dance, but Wendy missed the flash of something - worry? sadness? - that crossed his face. Instead, she closed her eyes and let herself be carried away by the music, secure in the knowledge that no matter what changed in her life, she would always have this: her best friend, awful throwing skills and all.

Chapter Three: Games People Play

"Oh. My. God." Mitch's horror-struck expression was reflected infinitely in the gleaming surfaces of Tiffany & Co.'s display cases. "Please tell me this is some sort of elaborate practical joke."

The china pattern Wendy had selected sat innocently on its velvet display cushion, all delicate scrollwork and gold trim. To Mitch, it looked like Marie Antoinette had thrown up on a plate.

"Thank God I was out of town when you decided on this pattern," he declared, drawing himself up to his full height. "It's hideous!"

The clerk behind the counter - a perfectly coiffed woman whose pearl necklace probably cost more than Mitch's monthly rent - looked thoroughly befuddled. She clearly wasn't used to such dramatic pronouncements in her carefully curated kingdom of crystal and china.

Wendy just smirked, completely unfazed by her best friend's theatrical display of disgust. After all, this was the same man who'd once staged a funeral for a houseplant she'd accidentally killed. "Nobody said you have to eat off them then!"

"But think of your future dinner guests!" Mitch pressed his hand to his heart. "Think of the children!"

"I think the children will survive," Wendy laughed, signing the final paperwork for her registry. "Besides, Bruce loves it."

"Bruce," Mitch muttered under his breath, "thinks wearing brown shoes with a black belt is acceptable."

Later that evening, safely ensconced in Mitch's carefully decorated condo (which had been featured in *San Francisco Home* last spring, a fact he managed to work into every conversation), they settled in for their traditional Sunday night Scrabble match. The fireplace cast a warm glow across the room as they arranged their tiles, mugs of cocoa steaming beside them. Mitch's golden retrievers sitting by his feet.

Wendy studied her letters with the intensity of a chess master. "O-X-Y-M-O-R-O-N," she spelled out triumphantly. "Oxymoron."

"Oh yeah," Mitch nodded appreciatively. "Like 'Peace Keeping Missiles?'"

"Or how about," Wendy grinned, "'Straight-Acting Gay Man!'"

"Otherwise spelled *'How you doing*?'" Mitch gave his best Joey Tribbiani impression and reached for his cocoa, decorated with the perfect swirl of whipped cream and cinnamon. "So, how many points did you get?"

Wendy looked them over carefully, dragging out the moment just to torture him. "Let's see. Triple word score, plus triple letter score on the X of course..."

"Of course," Mitch echoed dryly.

"Plus, fifty points for using all my letters. That's one hundred and thirty-seven points."

Mitch wrote down the score with the kind of grudging respect usually reserved for worthy adversaries. Ten years of Sunday night Scrabble matches, and she still managed to surprise him.

"So did I win?"

"Yeah," he admitted. "But only 'cause I let you."

Wendy sipped her cocoa and smiled into the soft blaze of the fire, looking perfectly content. The flames highlighted the strawberry-gold of her hair, reminding Mitch of all the nights they'd spent just like this - playing games, sharing secrets, building a friendship that defied every conventional boundary.

"So," he ventured after a moment, "when's he getting back?"

Wendy glanced breezily at her watch, but Mitch caught the tiny flutter of anticipation in the gesture. "Oh, I don't know. He may already be back at my place waiting for me now."

A heavy sigh escaped Mitch as he forced himself up off the carpet, away from their cozy scene of Scrabble and cocoa. "Well, we wouldn't want to keep ole lover boy waiting, now would we?"

"I really wish you could at least try to get along with him," Wendy said softly as she stood up. "I was hoping we could all hang out and do stuff together after the wedding."

Mitch rolled his eyes as he helped her with her coat. "Oh, gee, just what I always wanted, a menage a whaaaa!"

Seeing the genuine distress on Wendy's face, he softened his expression. "Oh, alright. I'll try. If you love him, he can't be all bad."

"Thank you."

"It's just tough for me to be friendly with a guy who is so uncomfortable around me, ya know?"

"He's only uncomfortable because he barely knows you!" Wendy protested. "He didn't grow up around gay people like I did. Anyway, I want you and Kevin to be our first official dinner guests as a married couple."

"You're ordering in I hope? Please tell me we won't have to eat off of those ugh, plates?" Mimicking gagging.

"Wise guy."

She glanced around the condo as she gathered her things, taking in the perfectly arranged throw pillows, the artfully placed coffee table books, the photos of their adventures together over the years. "Hey! Speaking of

Kevin, when is your knight in shining armor getting back from his trip?"

A dreamy smile crossed Mitch's face. "Hmm, come to think of it, he should have been home by now. Knowing him, he probably stopped off to buy me some white roses."

"Awwww...."

"Hey! I'm worth it!"

Watching Wendy head down the hallway toward her waiting fiancé, Mitch couldn't shake the feeling that something was off. Maybe it was the way Bruce had been acting lately, or maybe it was just his own prejudices clouding his judgment.

Either way, he hoped he was wrong. After all, Wendy deserved her fairy tale ending, even if it came with questionable taste in china.

Chapter Four: The Space Between

The scent of orange juice and Calvin Klein cologne greeted Wendy as she opened the condo door. Bruce stood in the kitchen, casual in his designer jeans and button-down, looking exactly like the man she'd fallen in love with three years ago when they literally bumped into each other at a baseball game. Two weeks without him had felt like forever.

"Oh boy, did I miss you like crazy!"

She launched herself into his arms with the kind of abandon that would have made her mother tsk about proper lady-like behavior. Their kisses tasted of citrus and longing, passionate enough to make up for fourteen days of separation. These were the moments Wendy lived for - when Bruce let his carefully maintained corporate facade slip away and was simply hers.

"The feeling is most definitely mutual," he murmured against her hair. "This lawyer guy I was traveling with was getting sick and tired of hearing about you all the time."

They settled onto the plush leather couch, Bruce's shoulders relaxing under her practiced massage. She'd learned early in their relationship that the quickest way to break through his professional armor was through his perpetually tense shoulders.

"Good! So, when do I get to meet him anyway? Is he coming to the wedding?"

The muscles under her fingers tensed again. "Oh right! Like we need one more person at this wedding!"

"True. But you've hardly invited anyone. If you want him there--"

"Right." Bruce's tone carried an edge she couldn't quite read. "I could just skip the meal so he can come."

Her hands stilled mid-massage. "Honey!"

"I'm kidding! Alright?" He closed his eyes, trying to recapture the moment. "Resume massage please..."

"Oh, no," Wendy said softly. "It's my turn."

Later that night at The Slider Cafe, their favorite date spot in North Beach, the tension had mostly melted away. They shared a corner booth, feeding each other bites of their meals and laughing like the happily almost married couple they were supposed to be. Bruce was in full storytelling mode, his eyes dancing with amusement.

"...so then he got so fed up that our food was taking so long, he whips out his cell and calls the restaurant." Bruce leaned forward, clearly enjoying himself.

"The waitress picks up as she's yakking away, flirting with this young guy at the counter, and he says 'Is this the blonde waitress named DeDe?' She gets all nervous and goes, 'Uh, yeah.' He says 'I'm the guy starving to death waiting for my food.' Then she sees him waving and gets all apologetic. We got our food with a complimentary dessert a minute later."

Wendy's laughter came easily, though something nagged at the back of her mind. The way Bruce talked about this mystery lawyer friend seemed different somehow - more animated, more engaged than his usual business trip stories.

"This guy sounds like a hoot. I can't wait to meet him."

"Yeah, he's a great guy. Pretty crazy, but when you're traveling around to meet with all these uptight real estate types, you gotta have a little fun, you know?"

She squeezed his hand across the table, feeling the familiar warmth of his skin against hers. He squeezed back, but something flickered across his face - so brief she might have imagined it.

"So, tell me about your two weeks without me," he said, his tone playful but with an undercurrent she couldn't quite place. "I know, it was probably brutal. Did you sit around all day just thinking of me, pining away..."

Wendy's eyebrows shot up. "Actually, I had a ball! Mitch kept me entertained the whole time."

The change in Bruce's expression was subtle but unmistakable - a tightening around his eyes, a slight downturn of his mouth. The same look he always got at the mention of her best friend. Wendy chose to forge ahead, pretending not to notice.

"His lover was out of town too, so we were both, what was the phrase he used? 'Workaholic Widows!' That's it. So we kept each other company."

The tension at their table was suddenly thick enough to cut with a knife. Bruce's jaw tightened in that way that always meant he was holding something back. Wendy backpedaled quickly.

"I was only kidding."

"Huh? What?" Bruce's attention seemed miles away, lost in thoughts she couldn't access.

"That joke. About being a workaholic widow."

"Oh, I know."

But he didn't know, not really. He couldn't understand the easy friendship she shared with Mitch, couldn't see past his own discomfort to recognize how special it was. Wendy pushed her food around her plate, wondering why her perfect reunion dinner suddenly felt so off-kilter.

Maybe it was just pre-wedding jitters, she told herself. After all, in less than a week, they'd be husband and wife, and everything would fall into place.

Wouldn't it?

34

Chapter Five: Roses and Dreams

The golden retrievers, Donny and Marie, dozed contentedly by the fireplace as their humans created their own pocket of warmth on the plush rug beside them. Mitch's condo looked like a high-end flower shop had exploded inside it - white roses filled every available surface, their sweet fragrance mixing with the cedar smoke from the fire and the rich aroma of the aged brie they were sharing.

Mitch nestled deeper into Kevin's embrace, savoring the peaceful moment. "Hmmmm, thanks again for the roses. How did you know?"

Kevin's chest rumbled with quiet laughter. "Gee. It could have been the subtle hints you dropped before I left. Or the half dozen text messages on the subject in the last forty-eight hours."

"Surely not that many!" Mitch sat up, genuinely aghast. He prided himself on his subtlety, after all. It was one of his many charms, along with his impeccable taste in window displays and his ability to pair the perfect wine with any meal.

"You're right," Kevin conceded, eyes twinkling. "Maybe only five."

Mitch playfully nudged him with his shoulder. "Which is perfectly reasonable, given how long you were gone." He took another sip of the Cabernet they were sharing, a vintage he'd been saving for Kevin's return.

"I'll bet you barely missed me -- with Wendy getting married in six days. I'm sure you guys hung out the entire time."

Something in Kevin's tone made Mitch study his face more carefully. Was that a hint of jealousy? But no, Kevin had always understood his friendship with Wendy. It was one of the things Mitch loved most about him.

"Yeah," he said softly. "I can hardly believe she's getting married, though."

"Ditto. Didn't Bruce tell her when they met that he didn't believe in marriage?"

Mitch sat up straighter, his wine forgotten. "Yeah. He called it an 'outdated patriarchal institution that insinuated that women were just property.' But you know he just picked that up out of some Betty Friedan book." The words came out more bitter than he'd intended. Donny, sensing his tension, lifted his head and whined softly.

"Why's he doing it then?"

"Wendy can be very persuasive." Mitch shrugged, but his mind was racing with all the things he wished he could tell his best friend about her fiancé.

"Ironic, isn't it?" Kevin mused.

"What?"

"That Bruce has to practically be dragged to the altar, while both of us would give anything to have our union and our love recognized."

The fire popped and crackled in the silence that followed. Mitch's voice, when he finally spoke, was heavy with emotion. "Some people just don't realize how fortunate they really are. I mean, here we are living in the most supposedly free country in the world, and yet we're not free to express our love for each other."

"Someday, baby!" Kevin tousled Mitch's perfectly styled hair, trying to lighten the mood. Marie thumped her tail against the floor in approval. "So, what would be your idea of a fantasy wedding?"

"One that's legal!" He smirked.

They both laughed, but there was a bittersweet edge to it that even the dogs seemed to sense, pressing closer to their humans in comfort. Kevin pressed on, determined to keep things playful. "No, really. Tell me."

"Well, let's see..." Mitch's eyes took on that dreamy quality they got whenever he was planning something spectacular, the same look that had earned him three consecutive "Best Holiday Display" awards at Nordstrom. "White roses..."

"Surprise!" Kevin gestured grandly to their flower-filled surroundings.

"Continuing... a horse-drawn carriage..."

"Princess Diana would be so proud."

"Linda Eder serenading me..."

"Ahhhh, nice choice."

"Medieval motif for the reception."

"Again, Princess Diana - with a dash of Camelot."

"And of course," Mitch turned to face him, blue eyes sparkling in the firelight, "you on my arm, fair Prince!"

Kevin leaned over and kissed him softly, tasting of wine and promises. "Of course."

They settled back into comfortable silence, the fire burning low as San Francisco's famous fog rolled in outside their windows. Donny and Marie had fallen back asleep, their gentle snoring providing a counterpoint to the crackling flames. It was the kind of perfect moment Mitch wished he could bottle up and save - just in case the nagging feeling he had about Bruce and Wendy's wedding turned out to be more than just paranoia.

But that was tomorrow's problem. Tonight, surrounded by white roses and wrapped in Kevin's arms, he would let himself dream of horse-drawn carriages and medieval receptions, of a world where love was just love, no qualifiers needed. After all, if Wendy could have her fairy tale wedding, why couldn't he at least dream of his own?

Chapter Six: The Dream Unravels

The "I Love Lucy" laugh track provided an ironically cheerful backdrop as Wendy and Bruce sat in bed, sharing their traditional post-lovemaking bowl of Rocky Road ice cream. Lucy's latest scheme was unfolding on the TV screen, but Bruce's attention was fixed on Wendy, watching as she smiled and licked chocolate from her spoon, completely unaware that her own world was about to implode.

His heavy sigh cut through Ricky Ricardo's exasperated Spanish. Wendy turned to him, ice cream forgotten. "Bruce, honey, what's the matter?"

He stroked her hair, still mussed from their earlier passion, and pressed a gentle kiss to her forehead. The tenderness of the gesture made what he was about to do even worse. "God, Wendy, I love you so much."

"I love you too!"

"With all your heart?"

Something in his tone made her stomach clench. "Of course with all my heart! Why, what's going on?" She set the ice cream bowl on the nightstand, suddenly not hungry at all.

"So, my little Wendy darling," he began, using the pet name that usually made her melt, "if we truly love each other, why do we have to have a wedding?"

Wendy sat bolt upright, the sheets pooling around her waist. "What?!"

"Why do we need a wedding?" Bruce pressed on, as if he hadn't just dropped a bomb into their perfect evening. "I mean, Goldie Hawn and Kurt Russell have been together for years without getting married, and they're very happy!"

"Yeah!" Wendy's voice rose an octave. "They also have two homes in Aspen! What's your point?"

"Really? I thought they sold one. Hmph." Bruce shook his head. "My point is, I just don't think we need a wedding to prove our love for one another. It all seems so... commercial!"

"So is Christmas. You've never had any trouble celebrating that." Ice crept into her tone, replacing the warmth from their earlier intimacy.

"Look Wendy, you know I love you. I've just never been into all of this... wedding stuff. You know that."

The phrase 'wedding stuff' hit her like a slap. She jumped up in bed, rage coursing through her veins. "Wedding *stuff*? Wedding *STUFF*?! This so-called wedding *STUFF* has cost my father nearly fifty thousand dollars! And that's even after we cancelled the bridesmaids parachuting into the reception."

"Don't you see? That's my point! Why should our love for one another have to cost anyone anything?"

"Well darling," Wendy's voice dripped with frustrated sarcasm, "it's a little late to worry about that now. The wedding is only six days away!"

"I've tried to bring this up before, but you wouldn't listen!" Bruce ran his hands through his hair, messing up his usually perfect coif. "I know it's been your dream to have a big wedding, but, I... I don't think I can go through with it. It's just not what I want."

"It's just cold feet, dear. They'll thaw out by Saturday." She tried for soothing, but her voice trembled.

"No, it's much more than that! I'm not nervous about spending my life with you -- I'm looking forward to that. I just don't believe in the necessity of a wedding."

"The necessity of it?" Wendy felt tears threatening but held them back. "The necessity is that it's a testimony of our love before all of our family and loved ones -- and God! I'd like us to be blessed in our union -- the way it's been done since Adam and Eve!"

Bruce shook his head as he climbed out of bed and started gathering his clothes. "I just can't go through with this, Wendy. Can't you respect my wishes?"

"Can't you respect *my* wishes?" The words came out childish and demanding, and she regretted them instantly. Bruce finished dressing and moved to the door, his expression hardening.

"Gee, and I thought this was supposed to be about us?"

"What's that supposed to mean?"

"Clearly, it's only about you. You want to have this wedding for your father, or for your friends, or for yourself. But not for us!"

"If you back out of this, there is no 'us.'" The words hung in the air between them like shattered glass.

"We don't need a piece of paper to prove we're in love! I don't buy it! I never have!"

Wendy pulled the covers up higher, suddenly feeling vulnerable in more ways than one. Her voice came out smaller than she intended. "We're getting married on Saturday, Bruce!"

He opened the door, the hallway light creating a harsh silhouette. "Maybe you're getting married on Saturday! But I'm not gonna be there!"

"What are you nuts?! Everybody we know is coming to this wedding!"

"Maybe I am nuts. But I'll tell you this much -- if you're planning on going through with this, you're going to have to find yourself another groom, 'cause I quit!"

The door slammed behind him with a finality that echoed through her bones. "Maybe I'll do just that!" she shouted after him, her voice breaking on the last word.

In the sudden silence, Lucille Ball's laughter continued to spill from the TV, a mocking soundtrack to the destruction of Wendy's perfect world. The Rocky Road ice cream melted forgotten on her nightstand, just like her dreams of a fairy tale wedding were melting away before her very eyes.

She reached for her phone, fingers hovering over Mitch's number, but stopped. What could she possibly say? How could she tell her best friend that the wedding he'd been helping her plan, the celebration of love he couldn't legally have himself, was falling apart because her fiancé just didn't "*believe*" in it?

On the TV screen, Lucy and Ricky's latest crisis was resolving itself with hugs and kisses. But Wendy knew that real life didn't work that way. Sometimes Prince Charming turned out to be a frog after all, and no amount of kissing could change that.

Chapter Seven: Desperate Times

The bridal shop's three-way mirror reflected Wendy from every angle as the seamstress made final adjustments to her dream wedding dress. The ivory silk caught the light perfectly, the beading sparkled just so, and the train... well, the train was absolutely perfect. Everything was perfect except for one tiny detail: she had no groom to marry.

Mitch lounged on the boutique's plush settee, watching his best friend pretend that her world wasn't crumbling around her perfectly coiffed head. "Boy, I admire you."

"How so?"

"You're the only bride I know that's ever walked down the aisle with no groom waiting at the end."

Wendy caught his eye in the mirror. "Hmmmm, that does pose a slight problem, doesn't it?"

"Slight? No. Problem? Yes."

"I don't care!" Wendy's chin lifted defiantly. "I won't let him ruin my fantasy wedding! The nerve of him! Implying that I was being selfish."

"Imagine that!" Mitch's tone was dry enough to rival the Mojave. "Now, seriously, what are you going to do?"

"I'll think of something." Wendy twisted to examine the back of the dress, as if the answer might be hidden in its perfect seams. "I just need to find myself another groom before Saturday!"

"Hey! You could always use my '*MR. INFLATABLE DATABLE*!'"

"Ewww! Gross!" But then something sparked in Wendy's eyes. "Wait a minute! How tall is he?"

"I wouldn't know," Mitch mischievously mused, "I've never seen him standing up."

There was a pause as Wendy giggled and turned from the mirror, studying Mitch with an appraising eye that made him suddenly nervous. Her gaze traveled from his shoulders - which just happened to be exactly Bruce's width - down to his perfectly polished shoes.

"Hey! You know, you'd fit into Bruce's tux just about perfectly..."

Their eyes met, and in that moment, a completely insane idea passed between them. The kind of idea that could only make sense to two people who'd spent the last decade getting each other out of increasingly ridiculous situations. Mitch's answering grin was equal parts terror and excitement.

Later that night, in the familiar comfort of his condo, Mitch mixed drinks with slightly shaky hands as Kevin arrived home from work. The familiar sound of his boyfriend's keys in the door made his heart race - or maybe that was just the panic setting in about what he was about to propose.

"We're going to a wedding Saturday!" Mitch announced, handing Kevin his perfectly mixed Manhattan.

"I thought it was canceled!"

"It was. This is *my* wedding."

Kevin nearly dropped his drink, amber liquid sloshing dangerously close to the rim. "What the hell are you talking about?"

"Well, I felt really bad for Wendy and all, so I'm going to be kind of like a stand-in for Bruce."

"Kind of like a stand-in for Bruce?! Have you lost your mind?"

"Oh come on, it'd be a shame to have all that shrimp go to waste!"

"You're not serious!"

"Sure. Why not?"

Kevin set his drink down carefully, as if handling explosives. "Gee... I don't know. Maybe the fact that you're gay. Wouldn't you be mocking marriage, just like the religious right is always accusing us of doing?"

"That's only when we want to marry each other." Mitch's attempt at humor fell flat. "They don't seem to mind if we marry straight women. Anyway, this would just be for fun. And then I'd get to go to Hawaii on the honeymoon. I have vacation time coming anyway."

"This is very weird. I mean, does she need a green card or something?"

"Please, she was born in Boston!"

"I thought you were going to take the plunge with me." The hurt in Kevin's voice made Mitch cross the room quickly, pulling him into his arms.

"I am! As soon as the voters decide we're entitled to equal rights. In the meantime, I'm just doing this to help her out. Everything's already planned and paid for." He pressed closer, feeling Kevin start to soften. "It'll be like a big party, and she said we can keep half the gifts!"

Kevin couldn't help but laugh, drawing Mitch in for a kiss. "Yeeha! Well, as long as you won't be deflowering the bride."

"Nah! You're the only one I want to deflower."

As they melted into playful kisses, Mitch tried to ignore the voice in his head suggesting that maybe, just maybe, this wasn't his most brilliant plan ever. But what else could he do? Wendy had been there for him through everything - coming out to his parents, his first major heartbreak, even that unfortunate bleached hair phase in '95. Now she needed him, and if that meant putting on a tux and pretending to be straight for one day... well, he'd certainly done worse things in the name of friendship.

Besides, what could possibly go wrong?

Chapter Eight: Family Matters

"Mom? Bruce called off the wedding!"

Wendy's announcement landed like a bomb in the Chilton household, where her mother Ellen was in the middle of her nightly face mask routine and her father Fred was reviewing what he fondly called his "wedding damage report" - otherwise known as his credit card statement.

"Bruce called off the wedding!" Ellen's voice reached a pitch typically reserved for opera sopranos.

There was a crash, followed by the sound of Fred picking up the extension. "What the hell do you mean Bruce called off the wedding?"

"Now Fred, remember your blood pressure!"

"To hell with my blood pressure! Remember my Visa bill!"

Wendy took a deep breath, reminding herself that she was the calm, rational one in the family. "Daddy, it's okay. The wedding's still on."

"Wait... so, Bruce came around?"

"Not exactly. I'm still getting married Saturday, but... not to Bruce."

"Huh?" her parents chorused in perfect unison.

"Remember my friend Mitch? He's going to step in."

There was a long pause before Fred spoke. "I thought he was a fruit loop!"

"Now, Fred, you know the church said to call them 'heterosexually-challenged.'"

"Whatever you call them, I thought it meant they don't like girls?"

"It's true, Mitch is heterosexually challen... gay, but--"

"Do you love him, dear?" Ellen interrupted, her voice taking on that soothing tone she usually reserved for convincing Fred to try her latest health food experiments.

"Well, of course, he's my--"

"Then that's all that matters."

"But what if the kids turn out like *that*?" Fred sputtered.

"Daddy! We're not going to--"

"Don't worry, Fred, I think Oprah says it often skips a generation."

"Mom! Dad! You're missing the point!"

"That's right, we are," Ellen agreed cheerfully. "Well, thanks for the update, dear."

"Yeah. We'll see you on Saturday. Don't be late."

The dial tone buzzed in Wendy's ear as she stared at the phone, wondering if she'd somehow slipped into an alternate dimension where her parents' complete misunderstanding of the situation actually made sense.

Across town, Mitch was having his own family moment, phone on speaker as he paced his living room. Kevin watched nervously from the couch, pretending to read while actually monitoring what promised to be another classic Mitch-and-Mother conversation.

"Your dime," Theresa answered, the sound of dishes clinking in the background.

"Hello Mother!"

"Mitch, my sweet perfect little angel! What's new pumpkin?"

"Well Mom, I'm getting married!"

"What??? To whats-his-name?"

"Kevin. And no. I'm marrying a woman."

The dish-washing sounds stopped abruptly. "Wait! A real woman? Not one of those Transvesalvania-thingy-ma-jiggys?"

"Transgender? No, Mom. I'm marrying someone who was born a woman."

The sound of over dramatic sobbing filled the line. "Oh Mitch, your father would be so happy if he were alive today..."

Mitch sighed. "Mom, Dad is alive. I just got off the phone with him."

"Hey, you have your fantasies, I have mine!"

Kevin stifled a laugh as Mitch rolled his eyes heavenward. "So, will you come to the wedding on Saturday?"

"Wait a minute! Wait just an Ellen DeGeneres minute here. You told me in that National Coming Out Day video years ago that you were gay and that you couldn't change."

"I am. I can't."

"What does whats-his-name think about all this?"

"He doesn't mind as long as I don't actually fool around with the bride. So, you're coming aren't you?"

"Hey, is this like one of those situations I saw on Geraldo where you guys can get all the rights that a gay couple could never have, like insurance, and all that stuff? 'Cause if it is, you can tell me. I'm pretty hip."

"No, mom. It's Wendy. You know her. I'm doing it for a toaster oven -- and the honeymoon trip to Hawaii."

"Um, okaaaaay. And does she know that whats-his-name is included in the dowry?"

"Yes, of course."

"Wow! Now that's a liberated woman."

As Mitch continued to navigate his mother's particular brand of logic, Kevin's cell phone buzzed. The caller ID made his blood run cold. Bruce. Their conversation was brief, hushed, but by the time both calls ended, the room felt charged with secrets.

"Mother Theresa is coming!" Mitch announced triumphantly.

"That's great. Listen, my new client just called. He's having some kind of crisis."

Mitch checked his watch. "A real estate crisis at this hour?"

"Not a work crisis -- something in his personal life."

"Since when are you his therapist?"

"Well, sort of since we were stuck together for two weeks on the road. We bonded."

"You barely know this guy! You told me you kept having to change pronouns because you didn't think he'd be cool about you being gay. So now--"

Kevin took a deep breath. "It's Bruce."

The name hung in the air between them like a live wire.

"What's Bruce?"

"My new client."

"This guy is also named Bruce?"

"No. This guy IS Bruce. Our Bruce. Or rather, Wendy's Bruce."

The truth spilled out then - about the business trip, about Kevin becoming Bruce's confidant while carefully hiding his own identity, about the advice he'd given that *may* have contributed to Bruce's wedding cold feet. With each revelation, Mitch's expression grew more incredulous.

"So instead of telling him you were the boyfriend of his fiancé's best friend, I became, what? Mitchelina?"

"Actually... Angelina."

"Angelina?"

"It's a compliment! You know how much I love her."

As their argument unfolded, the full weight of the situation settled over them. Kevin had inadvertently helped convince Bruce to back out of the wedding. Bruce had no idea his new friend was dating his ex-fiancé's gay best friend who was now planning to marry said ex-fiancé. You got that? And somewhere in the city, both sets of parents were preparing for a wedding that was either a complete farce or the most progressive ceremony

San Francisco had ever seen, depending on who you asked.

"I have to tell Wendy," Mitch declared, reaching for the phone.

Kevin's hand shot out to stop him. "Please don't! I don't want her to blame me."

"Why would she blame you? It's not like you told him to cancel the wedding."

Kevin's guilty silence spoke volumes.

"Oh my God, you didn't!"

"No, of course not! Well, not exactly. I just... encouraged him to stand up for himself."

"Do you have some kind of death wish?"

In the end, they struck a deal. Kevin would try to fix things with Bruce, and if he succeeded, he'd take Mitch to Hawaii and buy them a new toaster oven. If he failed... well, San Francisco was about to witness the most unique wedding in its history. And considering this was San Francisco, that was really saying something.

As Kevin headed out to meet Bruce, Mitch collapsed onto the couch, wondering how his simple act of friendship had turned into a romantic comedy worthy of a Lifetime movie.

Somewhere across town, his mother was probably already planning what to wear to her gay son's straight wedding, while Wendy's parents debated the genetic implications of their future grandchildren's sexual orientation.

At least the cake would be fabulous.

Chapter Nine: Last Call

The bar smelled of stale beer and missed opportunities. Bruce sat hunched in a corner booth, surrounded by empty glasses that reflected his fractured state of mind. When Kevin slid into the seat across from him, he barely looked up.

"Hey, dude. What's going on?"

Bruce lifted his head, his usual polished appearance decidedly rumpled. His tie hung loose around his neck like a surrender flag.

"I think I blew it. I decided to be completely honest with Wendy about how I felt -- and she freaked out! I think she broke up with me."

"You think?" Kevin tried to keep his voice neutral, fighting the urge to grab Bruce by his expensive shirt collar and shake some sense into him. After all, this mess was partly his fault.

"Nothing's clear right now." Bruce ran a hand through his hair, messing it up further. "I know I love her. But I also know this whole marriage thing is just a load of bull."

"Not to her though, right?" Kevin watched his client - his friend? - struggle with the concept that other people's feelings might matter as much as his principles.

"Yeah, but if I go crawling back now, what kind of message does that send?" Bruce's voice took on a defensive edge. "I don't want to be one of those wimpy guys who have to check with their wives before they can wipe their own butts!"

Kevin thought about all the compromises he and Mitch had made over the years, the daily negotiations of any real relationship. He thought about hiding who he was at work, about Mitch accepting that choice even though he hated it. He thought about Wendy, who'd probably spent her whole life dreaming of this wedding, only to have it dismissed as "a load of bull" by the man who claimed to love her.

"Would you rather be that lonely bachelor guy who eats ravioli out of a can every night because he let the right girl get away?"

"I thought you said I needed to stand up for myself?" The accusation in Bruce's tone was clear.

"You do." Kevin leaned forward, trying to find the words to undo the damage his previous advice had caused. "Now it's time to apologize and get married as planned."

Bruce stared into his empty glass, as if the answers might be hiding at the bottom.

Finally, he shook his head. "Nah. If she really loves me, she won't force me to do something I don't want to do!"

The irony of the situation wasn't lost on Kevin. Here he was, trying to save a straight wedding when he couldn't even have one of his own. And now Bruce, who had the right to marry anyone he loved, was throwing it away over what? Pride? Fear? A misguided stand against "the institution of marriage" that conveniently ignored the fact that millions of people, including Kevin himself, were still fighting for that very right?

He thought about Mitch, probably at home right now planning how to turn Wendy's traditional wedding into something that would make the Pride parade look understated. He thought about the look on Wendy's face when she realized her fiancé valued his principles more than her happiness. He thought about his own closeted life, and how sometimes love meant doing things that scared you.

But Bruce was already signaling for another drink, clearly done listening to reason. Kevin watched him, wondering if this was karma for all the times he'd chosen his career over being honest about who he was. Maybe some people had to learn their lessons the hard way.

One thing was certain - Saturday's wedding was going to be interesting, with or without the original groom.

Chapter Ten: Mixed Signals

The Chilton's' immaculate living room was in a state of barely controlled chaos as Ellen and Fred rushed to get ready for the grand opening of the new Bingo-Bowlarama-Dome. Ellen was adjusting her lucky bingo visor when the phone rang.

"Ah, hello?" Ellen wedged the phone between her ear and shoulder while searching for her favorite dauber.

"Ellen? It's Janice, Bruce's mother."

Ellen froze, her visor slightly askew. Janice Hollingsworth's perfectly modulated voice could make even a grocery list sound like a social judgment.

"Oh, hello dear. I'm sorry, but we're just rushing out the door. The new Bingo-Bowlarama-Dome is finally having its grand opening."

"My, how exciting." Janice's tone suggested it was anything but. "I only called to share my grievances about the cancellation of the wedding. You know those crazy kids of ours--"

Fred was already by the door, making frantic "hurry up" gestures. The early bird special waited for no one, not even social obligations to the almost-in-laws.

"Oh, no," Ellen cut in brightly. "We spoke to Wendy last night. The wedding is back on."

There was a pause on the other end. "Really? Why wasn't I informed?"

"Maybe because--"

Fred, deciding that free food trumped social niceties, grabbed the phone. "We can't talk now! We need to get there before all the free food is gone!"

The phone hit the cradle with a decisive click as Fred hustled Ellen toward the door, her protests about proper phone etiquette falling on deaf ears.

Dumbfounded in her tastefully appointed sitting room at Hollingsworth Manor in Santa Barbara, Janice stared at her phone as if it had personally offended her. After a moment's consideration, she dialed Bruce's number, only to be greeted by his answering machine's cheerful wedding-themed message.

The recording of her son's attempt at singing made her wince. Really? Had she paid for those voice lessons for nothing.

"Bruce darling, Mummy here. I'm a tad confused. I just spoke with Wendy's mother, and she said the wedding's on. I'm so glad you kids were able to work things out." She paused to examine her perfectly manicured nails. "I'm going to have to leave here in the morning with your Aunt Beatrice, she wants to drive up the coast and visit Carmel. Ugh! Do try and reach me before then, okay? Thanks darling. Big kiss. Ta-ta!"

As she hung up, Janice couldn't shake the feeling that something was off. The Chiltons had seemed almost... evasive. And since when did Ellen Chilton rush anywhere for bingo? The woman usually treated those games like military operations, arriving precisely forty-five minutes early with her lucky daubers arranged by color.

Still, if the wedding was back on, surely Bruce would have told her. Unless... No, her son wouldn't keep something this important from his own mother. Would he?

She glanced at the formal wedding invitation still displayed on her mantel, wondering if perhaps she should make a few more calls before packing for Carmel. After all, a mother had a right to know if her son was getting married on Saturday.

And to whom.

Chapter Eleven: Dress Rehearsal

"Well, what do you think, guys?"

Mitch executed a perfect runway spin in Ted's Tuxedo Shop, the kind he'd perfected during his stint as a department store window dresser. The tuxedo fit perfectly, though that was hardly surprising - he and Bruce had always been about the same size, a fact that was either cosmic irony or proof that the universe had a sense of humor.

Kevin shrugged, deliberately casual. "It's alright, I guess."

The disappointment on Mitch's face was quickly covered by his best friend Bob, who had come to the rescue to help with the 911 wedding plans, he swooped in to wrap an arm around his shoulders. "Don't mind her. She's just jealous 'cause she won't get to carry you over the threshold on your wedding night."

Mitch laughed while Kevin let out a grunt that suggested he wasn't finding any of this particularly amusing.

"I think you look ravishing!" Bob declared. "You belong on the top of a wedding cake... or better yet, the cover of *Gay Weddings* magazine!"

"Is there such a thing?"

"If there isn't, there should be!"

Kevin, clearly trying to maintain his role as the voice of reason, cut in. "So, have you and Wendy discussed who gets to throw the bouquet?"

"Or, more importantly," Bob added, "who gets to walk down the aisle?"

"Oh, that's easy." Mitch smoothed his lapels. "We decided that we'll walk down together."

Kevin and Bob exchanged a knowing grimace.

"Yeah, we figured we'd be non-traditional and make a political statement, walking side by side, as equals--"

"She wouldn't budge on the aisle thing, huh?"

"Not an inch!"

Later at Fabio's Florist, the reality of their unusual situation became even more apparent. The shop was a riot of color and fragrance, with Wendy and her maid of honor Cindy deep in consultation with Fabio when Mitch and Bob arrived. The quick peck Mitch gave Wendy's cheek was perfectly platonic, but it still made Kevin's absence feel more conspicuous.

"Sorry we're late," Mitch apologized.

"Yeah, Romeo here couldn't decide between the pink chiffon or the peach taffeta!" Bob's declaration earned a horrified look from Cindy.

"He's kidding," Mitch assured her quickly.

"It's okay. I was just explaining our little dilemma to Fabio." Wendy's smile was just a touch too bright. "Fabio, Cindy, this is the man I'm marrying on Saturday, Mitch."

They both nodded, clearly struggling to process this information.

"And this is his friend, Bob who's helping with the planning."

Bob seized Fabio's hand with enthusiasm. "And I hope I can be your friend, too!"

Fabio extracted his hand carefully, his thick Italian accent growing more pronounced with confusion. "Well, isn't that nice? Now, Wendy tells me you would like a bouquet to throw as well. Is this true?"

Mitch nodded, earning a head shake and dramatic sigh from the florist.

"Where I come from, two bouquets, they are bad luck."

"And where do you reign from, your highness?" Bob's tone dripped honey-coated acid.

"My point is this: it's not right what you are doing to this sacred thing of marriage. Marriage is a commitment between two people until death do them part."

"Or in the case of middle America, a mid-life crisis and a buxom blonde." Bob quipped.

"You know Wendy," Cindy jumped in, "Fabio has a point. Why don't you call Bruce? Work it out. This is crazy what you're doing." She glanced at Mitch apologetically. "No offense. But I mean, you're about to marry a gay man. Poor Mitch will become the poster boy for the sum total of why women never meet the right guy: they're either married or gay, and now in this case, both!"

"How surprisingly profound!" Bob mused.

"It's your call," Mitch told Wendy softly.

"Do you want to go through with it?" The uncertainty in her voice made something twist in Mitch's chest.

"Well, you're my best friend and I want to help you out, so..."

Bob's theatrical throat-clearing interrupted the moment. "I thought *I* was your best friend!"

"You are. Wendy's my best girl-friend."

Bob's look could have wilted the entire flower shop. "I thought *I* was your best girlfriend!"

"My best *girl* girlfriend. Okay?"

"Hmmmm... okay, I can live with that!" Bob was somewhat satisfied.

"So, Mitch, you're still in?" Wendy's amusement at their banter couldn't quite hide her vulnerability.

"If Bruce isn't there, then I will be." He straightened his shoulders. "Besides, I really need that toaster oven."

"Hey! The toaster oven is from me!" Cindy protested.

Standing there among the roses and lilies, surrounded by the trappings of traditional romance, Mitch couldn't help but appreciate the absurdity of their situation. Here he was, a gay man about to marry his best friend, while his closeted boyfriend tried to convince her runaway fiancé to come back, all because of a toaster oven and a dream wedding that was rapidly turning into something that would make even San Francisco raise its eyebrows.

But looking at Wendy's face, seeing the mix of hope and determination there, he knew he'd go through with it. After all, what were best friends for, if not to step in when Prince Charming turned out to be more of a frog than expected?

Besides, he really did want that toaster oven.

Chapter Twelve: Truth and Consequences

The coffee shop bustled with the usual morning crowd, but Bruce looked like he'd rather be anywhere else. His usually immaculate appearance was rumpled, dark circles under his eyes suggesting he'd been doing more drinking than sleeping. He winced at the clatter of dishes from behind the counter.

"Owwwww! My head hurts! I've been drinking way too much."

Kevin watched his client - his friend? His almost-brother-in-law? - struggle with his hangover and his conscience. The roles were getting harder to keep straight.

"You miss her, huh?"

"Of course I miss her! I love her." The raw honesty in Bruce's hoarse voice made Kevin's stomach twist with guilt.

"Then call her."

"And say what?"

Kevin leaned forward, choosing his words carefully. After all, he was partly responsible for this mess.

"Say you don't believe in the institution of marriage, but that you DO believe in her. And if going through with this wedding will make her happy, then that's what you'll do."

The words felt strange in his mouth, considering he'd spent the last two weeks encouraging Bruce to "stand up for himself." Now here he was, trying to undo the damage before his boyfriend had to actually go through with marrying his best friend. The whole situation felt like something out of a bad sitcom.

"It's too late. I'm sure she's already cancelled everything."

"No, she hasn't." The words slipped out before Kevin could stop them.

Bruce's puzzled look made him backtrack quickly. "I mean, I'm sure she hasn't. She's still hoping you'll change your mind and marry her."

"You sure seem to know a lot about women."

Kevin forced a smile, wondering what Bruce would think if he knew that "Angelina" was actually Mitch, who was currently being fitted in said grooms tuxedo to marry Wendy in Bruce's place.

"Well, my Angelina has always dreamed of the perfect wedding too."

Bruce stared into his coffee cup as if it might hold the answers he was looking for. "No. It's too late. The wedding is Saturday." His voice took on a practical tone that couldn't quite mask the regret underneath. "Wendy's a romantic, but she's also practical. She'd have done whatever she could to get her father's money back."

Kevin shook his head and sighed, defeated. He couldn't tell Bruce the truth without revealing his own deception. He couldn't stop the wedding without hurting Wendy even more. And he couldn't help feeling that this whole mess was karma catching up with him for staying in the closet at work.

The morning light streaming through the coffee shop windows caught Bruce's now abandoned wedding ring, which he'd been fidgeting with throughout their conversation. It sent little sparkles dancing across their table - nature's own cosmic irony, highlighting the symbol of a commitment Bruce had thrown away and Kevin couldn't legally make.

Some days, Kevin thought, the universe had a particularly twisted sense of humor.

Chapter Thirteen: The Show Must Go On

The reception hall echoed with music as three stunning drag performers rehearsed their number under Bob's direction. What they lacked in polish, they made up for in enthusiasm - at least until the bumping started.

"Alright! That's it! I can't work like this!" The first drag queen's voice dropped two octaves with indignation.

Bob rolled his eyes heavenward, silently counting to ten. "What now?"

"Ms. RuPaul-wannabe here won't stop bumping into me!"

"What you talking about? '*Ms. RuPaul-wannabe*?' I ain't no RuPaul-wannabe!"

The third queen couldn't resist joining the fray. "MmmHmmm. Then why do you spend half the day lip syncing every song she's ever done in front of the mirror?"

"That's Diana Ross, you heifer!"

"Like there's a difference?"

Their laughter echoed through the hall, but Bob was quickly losing patience with the diva dynamics.

"Well, girls, what do you suggest we do to fix the problem?"

Drag Queen number three stepped forward with the air of someone solving world peace. "Why don't I stand in the middle, and Ms. Diana Ross-wannabe can stand in my place. Cool?"

The rearrangement lasted exactly thirty seconds before another collision sent them back into chaos.

"That's it! I quit!"

As the other two queens chased after their fleeing sister, promising reconciliation, Bob slumped into a nearby chair. When Wendy had agreed to let him handle the entertainment, he'd promised her something unforgettable. He just hadn't specified whether that would be in a good way or a bad way.

The evening brought better fortune in the form of Mitch's surprise bachelor party. Their laughter echoed down the hallway as they worked the key in their condo's lock, completely unprepared for the crowd waiting inside.

"SURPRISE!"

The lights blazed on to reveal a room full of friends - the drag queens now in various states of drag and un-drag, familiar faces from their favorite clubs, and what looked like half of San Francisco's theater community.

Mitch turned to Kevin, eyes wide. "Did you know about this?"

Kevin's answering smile was all the confirmation needed.

"How do think we got the security code?" Bob called out. "I didn't know you could use dirty words for codes. You naughty naughty boys."

Both Kevin and Mitch blushed as Bob triumphantly waved a DVD. "I've never done this before.

But I did some research, and I found out that straight men get together and watch dirty movies and get drunk..."

The hoots and hollers that followed suggested this wasn't going to be your typical bachelor party. Then again, nothing about this wedding was typical. As their friends poured drinks and argued over movie selections, Mitch caught Kevin's eye across the room. Tomorrow he would be walking down the aisle with his best friend, while his boyfriend watched on while playing the role as his best man, still pretending to be straight to the man who should have been the groom.

But tonight wasn't about that. Tonight was about celebrating love in all of its complicated forms - even if that meant watching whatever questionable entertainment Bob had selected for his "research" into straight bachelor parties.

After all, if Mitch was going to pretend to be straight, he might as well learn from the experts.

Chapter Fourteen: The Last Night of Freedom

The glow from Mitch's TV cast flickering shadows across the faces of his increasingly inebriated guests. Toby lunged for the remote control; eyes gleaming. "Let's go back. I love this part!"

A chorus of protests erupted as Igor attempted to wrestle the remote away. "That's it! Give me the remote!"

Bob intervened with the practiced air of a kindergarten teacher breaking up a playground squabble. "Boys! Please! Control yourselves! I know this movie gets us all a little... passionate. But let's show a little decorum. I mean, reeeally!"

The culprits bowed their heads, mumbling apologies like chastised children.

"Alright then. May I turn the movie back on now?" Bob teased.

The resulting chorus of begging would have made a teen slumber party proud. As the film resumed, a moment of hushed anticipation filled the room. Then, as if on cue, everyone raised their wire hangers skyward and screamed hysterically.

"NO MORE WIRE HANGERS!!!"

Kevin and Bob exchanged indulgent looks as their friends brandished their makeshift weapons, *Mommie Dearest* providing the perfect soundtrack to their theatrical display.

The evening progressed to *All About Eve,* with a drinking game that had them taking shots every time Eve's name was mentioned. "Eeeew! Eve!" became progressively more slurred as the night wore on.

Just when it seemed the party might wind down, Bob stepped forward with a gleam in his eye. "Now, now. Just relax. I forgot to mention what the rest of my research revealed to me..."

The opening notes of "Thus Spake Zarathustra" filled the room as Bob made his announcement. "Mitch, may I present to you, the amazing Marco!"

The stripper who burst through the door looked like he'd stepped straight out of a leather fashion magazine. As Marco began his performance, gyrating around a thoroughly flustered Mitch, Bob couldn't resist one more surprise.

"Oh, yeah. I forgot. Since you're marrying a woman tomorrow -- and a lovely one she is -- I wasn't sure if you wanted one of these, to… you know, balance it out..."

Enter Lola, a vision in sequins and feathers, who promptly claimed Mitch's lap as her stage. Mitch's desperate glance toward Marco spoke volumes about his preferences, earning laughs from the assembled crowd.

Outside on the front steps, Kevin gulped in the cool night air, only to find Wendy approaching.

"Hey you. I just stopped by to see how the party was going."

He gestured toward the window. "Take a look for yourself."

She peeked in just in time to see both Marco and Lola vying for Mitch's attention. "It looks like he's having a good time!"

"Yeah. Well, what are you gonna do? That's Mitch."

"Listen, Kevin." Wendy joined him on the porch swing. "We've never really talked about all this. Are you alright with this whole arrangement?"

The swing creaked gently as Kevin considered his response. "Well, sure, I mean... it's kinda weird, but..."

"Yeah, I'll give you that. But, you know, he's only doing this for me." She paused. "And for the toaster oven and the trip to Hawaii." They both laughed. "What I mean is that he has been the best friend any dumped bride-to-be could ever have. I was upset about Bruce just walking out on me like that, and quite frankly, I didn't know what I was going to do. Mitch helped bring clarity to the situation and helped lighten the mood."

Kevin felt his conscience twinge. "Have you tried talking with Bruce?"

"He hasn't called."

"You could call him."

"He's the one who left -- he should call me!"

"I'm working on it," Kevin murmured.

"What do you mean?"

"Never mind. Look, I just hope going through with this wedding is the right thing."

"You mean for Mitch?"

"Oh, Mitch is in heaven. I meant for you."

Wendy's smile was soft as she hugged him. "You're really special you know? Mitch is a very lucky guy."

"Thanks." Kevin managed a smile. "So is Bruce -- if the dolt would just let go of his pride and realize it."

"You talk like you know him."

"I feel like I do." He cringed.

Above them, a fresh wave of laughter and music spilled from the windows. Wendy grinned. "I'll bet Mitch doesn't remember a bit of this tomorrow."

They shared a knowing look, but Kevin's smile didn't quite reach his eyes. In less than twenty-four hours, his boyfriend would be getting married to the woman whose fiancé he'd inadvertently counseled into leaving her. Somewhere in heaven, Oscar Wilde was probably taking notes.

Inside, Mitch was still caught between a stripper and their hard place, while his friends continued their enthusiastic yet questionable tribute to classic cinema. It was exactly the kind of chaos that had defined their friendship from the beginning - beautiful, messy, and completely impossible to explain to outsiders.

Tomorrow would bring whatever it would bring. But tonight was for celebrating, even if everyone was too drunk to quite remember what they were celebrating anymore.

Chapter Fifteen: Wedding Day Chaos

The morning of the wedding dawned with Mitch nursing what felt like the worst hangover in San Francisco history. As he struggled with his bow tie in the chapel's groom's room, his bleary eyes registered something unusual - a parade of extremely fit men wearing... well, not much at all.

"Hi!" The first Chippendale greeted him cheerfully, as casual as if he was dressed for a board meeting rather than wearing only tuxedo pants and a bow tie.

"Uh, hi there," Mitch managed, wondering if this was some sort of hangover hallucination.

Two more equally underdressed gentlemen appeared. "Hey! What's up?"

"Uh, hi. Uh, nothing much. You know... getting married." Mitch turned back to his reflection, questioning his life choices and exactly how much he'd had to drink last night.

Bob's appearance – colorfully resplendent in what appeared to be a formal nightgown – attempted to clarify matters.

"Bob? Could you come here for a minute?"

"Yes, my little groom-to-be?"

"Curious... uh, who are all these half-naked men running around the church? Choir boys? Not that I'm complaining"

Bob's confused expression matched his own. "Now that's funny! No honey. They're the ushers you asked for."

"Um... *I* asked for them?"

"You told me to call your buddies at Chippendale to be ushers!"

"NO! I asked you to call my buddies Chip *and* Dale! You know them -- they live in Noe Valley?"

Bob's hand flew to his mouth in theatrical shock. "Oooooopsy! Are you mad?"

"Nah. It's actually kinda funny. But they uh, do have more to wear, right?"

"Of course, darling! They have cummerbunds silly."

Meanwhile, in the bride's room, Wendy was putting the finishing touches on her perfect bridal look, surrounded by bridesmaids and family. Her mother Ellen breezed in, practically glowing with excitement.

"Well, I just met some of those nice young friends of Mitch who are ushers. Did you know they work for Chippendale?"

"Yes, we just found that out ourselves," Cindy replied diplomatically.

"It's so nice to see the youth of today take such an interest in handmade furniture," Ellen mused. "But honestly, who knew the company was still in business? Haven't they been making furniture since 1932?"

"Do you mean Ethan Allen Mrs. Chilton?" Cindy chimed in.

Wendy caught Cindy's eye in the mirror and shook her head slightly. Some battles weren't worth fighting.

The morning's relative calm shattered when Cindy pulled out her phone. "You know, it's not too late. You could still call Bruce. Talk him into it. Maybe your Dad could threaten him or something, right Mr. Chilton?"

"Will you all just lay off!" Wendy's voice carried more frustration than anger. "I don't want Bruce doing something he doesn't want to do! He loves me, and I love him, but he doesn't want a wedding, and I do. It's as simple as that. So can we just drop it, please?"

Ellen's hands settled on her daughter's shoulders, gentle but insistent. "Will Bruce still want to be with you after you marry someone else?"

The question hung in the air, unanswered and unavoidable.

Across town, Bruce was about to get his own wake-up call. Passed out on his couch surrounded by empty beer bottles, he barely registered his answering machine picking up Cindy's urgent message: "Bruce, it's Cindy. Are you there? You've got to do something to stop this insanity. Cold feet is one thing, but do you really want Wendy to marry another guy? Get your butt down here now!"

Bruce bolted upright, suddenly very awake. "What the hell?"

His attempt to call Wendy's cell went straight to voicemail. Without bothering to change or clean up, he grabbed his coat and ran for the door, leaving it swinging behind him.

The stage was set for either the most memorable wedding San Francisco had ever seen, or its most spectacular disaster.

Possibly both.

Chapter Sixteen: The Not-So-Perfect Wedding

San Francisco had seen its share of unique weddings, but even by local standards, this one was pushing boundaries. As guests arrived at the chapel, they were greeted by what appeared to be Barbra Streisand and Liza Minnelli - if Barbra and Liza had been six feet tall and blessed with bass voices.

"Bride or groom?" the Streisand impersonator inquired of Bruce's mother Janice, who looked like she'd just bitten into a particularly sour lemon.

"Uh, we are with the, uh, groom. I'm his mother."

"Oh, you must be so proud of our little Mitch!"

"Mitch? Who's Mitch?"

But Barbra was already whisking her and Aunt Beatrice to the second row, leaving them to take in the increasingly surreal scene. Beatrice's eyes widened at the parade of colorful guests filling the chapel.

"I had no idea Bruce had such colorful friends!"

"He doesn't!" Janice winced.

"And wow! Barbra Streisand! Why didn't you tell me he knew Barbra Streisand!"

The confusion only multiplied when Mitch's mother Theresa arrived and was posed the same question.

"Bride or groom?"

"I'm the mother of the groom."

"But I just sat the mother of the groom."

Theresa's face darkened with sudden fury. "Is that strumpet calling herself my son's mother? I'll kill her!"

Meanwhile, in a quiet chapel hallway, the bride and groom shared a private moment.

"Hey! Isn't it bad luck for you to see me before the wedding?"

"I think that only counts if we're not walking down the aisle together," Mitch replied, adjusting his boutonnière.

"So, are you nervous?"

"Nah....yeah. A little. I had a serious chat with your Dad."

"Welcome to the family."

"At least I have protection into the year 2030."

Wendy's laugh echoed off the chapel walls. "Sorry about that. Oh, I love your ushers by the way."

"Oh yeah? They weren't my idea, actually. I hope it doesn't ruin your fantasy wedding."

"No. Not at all. Who wouldn't want Barbra Streisand and Liza Minnelli at their wedding?"

"I think Bob was going for a *La Cage Aux Folles* motif."

"Mission accomplished."

The ceremony itself was a masterclass in controlled chaos. The procession began with the bridesmaids being escorted by half-naked Chippendales dancers, followed by Kevin and Cindy, then Bob as a bigger than life flower 'girl' dragging little Timmy, the terrified ring bearer behind him, and finally Wendy and Mitch, hand in hand, with their respective fathers flanking them like bewildered bodyguards.

When they reached the altar, the minister's expression suggested he was seriously reconsidering his career choices.

"Who gives this woman away?"

"I do," Fred answered firmly.

After a whispered consultation with Wendy, the minister added with only slight hesitation, "And, uh, who gives this man away?"

Walter Pratt shifted uncomfortably. "Uh, I, uh, do."

"You're not Bruce, are you?" the minister asked Mitch.

"Mitchell Conrad Pratt, sir," Mitch replied, offering a firm handshake.

"Very well then. Now that everything is in order, let's begin, shall we? First order of business... If there is anyone here who knows why these two should not be joined in holy matrimony, let them speak now or forever hold their peace."

The forest of raised hands that followed - including Kevin's and Cindy's - nearly caused the minister to drop his prayer book.

He turned to Wendy and Mitch, "It seems we may have a bit of opposition here."

What followed was perhaps the longest list of objections ever heard in a house of worship: "Because she's supposed to be marrying my son!" (Janice), "Because my son is gay!" (Theresa), "Yeah! He's *totally* gay!" one of the drag queens chimed in, and finally after what seemed like forever, one particularly passionate gay friend in the audience, "...and I don't think it's fair that they can get married just because she has a real vay-jay-jay, when my man and I can't!" The crowd murmured and shouted in agreement.

It wasn't until both bride and groom raised *their* hands that the minister found salvation in an alternative.

"Why don't you two just do a Commitment Ceremony? I do it for gay and lesbian couples all the time. Think of it as two best friends committing to be friends forever."

"That sounds ideal! Why didn't we think of that before?"

And so it was that Bruce arrived just in time to hear Wendy laughing "I do!" - not realizing it was for a ceremony celebrating friendship rather than marriage.

He watched from behind a tree as the happy couple emerged into a shower of rainbow sprinkles ("prettier than rice and it tastes better too!" according to Bob).

The photo session that followed captured it all for posterity: the bridesmaids with their Chippendale escorts, the best man kissing the groom, Bobbie-Girl towering over the terrified Timmy, and at the center of it all, Wendy and Mitch, their joy as real as their marriage wasn't.

Somewhere in heaven, Emily Post was probably having a fit. But this was San Francisco, where love - in all of its forms - had always made its own rules.

Chapter Seventeen: The Rainbow Reception

The reception hall looked like a medieval castle had collided with a Pride parade. Ornate tapestries hung alongside rainbow banners, while suits of armor stood guard over bars staffed by Chippendale dancers. It was exactly the kind of compromise you'd expect when a *fabulous* gay man and his best friend split decorating duties.

"I still don't understand why you made everyone else go home if we're staying?" Aunt Beatrice whispered to Janice, watching a particularly enthusiastic Chippendale mix martinis.

"Because, sister dear, I want to get to the bottom of this."

Ellen and Fred's approach interrupted their conspiratorial whispers. "Janice! What on earth are you doing here?"

"I assumed that my son was marrying your daughter."

"You know what happens when you assume," Fred offered helpfully.

"Fred, really!"

"So, you can imagine my mild disappointment when I saw your daughter trying to marry another man."

"Must have been quite a shocker!"

Across the room, another family drama was unfolding as Theresa dodged her ex-husband's attempts at reconciliation.

"Walter. Just stay away from me! The first time was only a warning. The next time I *will* run you over with my car!"

"Oh, come on, Terri. I'm sorry, okay? I was going through a mid-life crisis. I was stupid!"

"Then why didn't you just buy a new car, or a new hairpiece? Or better yet, do what I did -- get a makeover. It only cost me seventy-five dollars, not my marriage!"

The traditional wedding activities took on a new life under Bob's direction. When the Chicken Dance threatened to overtake the dance floor, he grabbed the microphone with a dramatic sigh.

"This is soooo heterosexual!"

"Well, what do you suggest?" Mitch asked, already dreading the answer.

"Ladies and Gentlemen. And others." Bob's announcement drew appreciative laughter. "I think it's time we did the 'CONGA!'"

A stunning Latina drag queen emerged to lead the charge, and soon even the resistant Janice found herself swept into the line, pushed by an enthusiastic Beatrice.

The father-daughter dance evolved into something uniquely their own when Bob insisted Walter join in on the tradition.

"Oh, no. No way!"

"Yes way!"

Soon both fathers were on the dance floor, Walter awkwardly swaying with Mitch while Fred twirled Wendy.

"Thanks for being part of this Dad. It's... surprisingly cool of you."

"Ah, well. I may not understand your life, but I love you and I just want you to be happy."

"Thanks, Dad."

When Fred playfully cut in, Walter shocked everyone by grabbing him for an impromptu waltz, complete with dramatic dips. Their laughter proved infectious as other couples joined the dance floor.

The cake presentation revealed yet another compromise - Wendy's elegant four-tiered creation in pristine white alongside Mitch's towering six-tier fluorescent pink and rainbow masterpiece, topped with a groom sporting a rainbow tuxedo.

"You just had to have more tiers than me," Wendy teased.

Mitch's innocent shrug fooled no one.

Kevin's best man speech brought the room to attention with the gentle ring of crystal.

"Greetings one and all. And thank you for coming. Since I am, technically, the best man at this uh, technical wedding of my lover. I guess that means I'll give the technical best man's speech -- technically."

The laughter encouraged him to continue. "Please forgive me for its crudity. I was only asked to do this five days ago, so I had to cram in a lot of research about our groom here."

"I've been very close to Mitch for over five years now. We've shared the same condo, the same toothpaste, and as a matter of fact..." He leaned into the microphone with a stage whisper, "...the same bed! Don't tell Wendy, I'm not sure if she knows."

The hoots and hollers made Theresa roll her eyes, but Kevin pressed on, pulling out a slip of paper. "So, with that in mind, I thought maybe I'd give his lovely new bride some tips about how to please her new mate, but then I thought, wait a minute! I've been doing everything on this list and look where it got me! Best man at my lovers wedding to a woman!"

His eyes rolled as laughter erupted when the crumpled paper hit the floor and Kevin's voice softened. "But I will tell the new bride a few things about her beloved. He is the most loving, caring and crazy individual on the face of the planet, and to join with him is to join with love. He has shown me nothing but compassion, hope, excitement, and great joy. And now," a big grin swept across his face as he motioned toward Mitch, "he's all yours sweetheart!"

More laughter, hoots and howls from the guests.

"Just remember -- he sleeps on the left side. He cooks a mean tuna casserole and keep those Abercrombie and Fitch catalogues out of the bathroom, or you'll never get him out of there!"

Raising his glass, Kevin's voice carried across the room. "A toast to the most beautiful bride... And the most handsome groom. To Wendy and Mitch!"

"To Wendy and Mitch!" the crowd echoed, glasses raised to this most unconventional of unions.

In that moment, surrounded by medieval tapestries and Chippendale bartenders, drag queens and disapproving relatives, something magical happened. The lines between friend and lover, family and chosen family, traditional and radical all blurred into something new and wonderful.

It wasn't the wedding anyone had planned, but somehow it had become exactly the celebration they all needed.

Chapter Eighteen:
Something Borrowed, Something Askew

The reception hall's front steps had become an impromptu stage for the traditional bouquet toss - or in this case, tosses. Fabio the florist watched with mounting horror as both bride and groom prepared to throw their flowers, no doubt wondering how his carefully crafted arrangements had ended up in this
situation.

Cindy caught Wendy's bouquet with practiced ease, but Mitch's throw turned into an inadvertent game of catch with his mother. The bouquet ping-ponged between them like a floral tennis match until Theresa finally intercepted it with a dramatic eye roll, marching over to Kevin.

"Here! You'll need this before I ever will."

"Thanks, Mother Theresa."

Her expression softened as she studied her son's partner.

"You really love my son, don't you?"

"Yes ma'am. More than anything in the world."

"Okay, okay. Don't get too graphic." But there was warmth in her mock disgust. "The point is. I love him, too. And I don't want him to get hurt."

"I would never hurt Mitch."

"Sure, that's what all men say. Look what happened to me and his father."

Kevin's eyes sparkled with mischief. "You can rest assured; I will never run off with a younger woman."

She swatted his shoulder but couldn't hide her growing affection. "Listen, you little wise guy! Just take good care of my baby, okay?"

"Okay. I will."

"Now come give your Mother Theresa a hug."

Their embrace, sealed with a kiss on Kevin's cheek, brought tears to Mitch's eyes as he watched from across the steps. Sometimes love came in unexpected packages.

Later that night, as Wendy packed for her unconventional

honeymoon, a knock at her door shattered her post-wedding glow. Bruce stood swaying slightly in her doorway, the smell of whiskey preceding him.

"Can I come in?"

She stepped aside, letting him stumble past.

"I can't believe you actually went through with the wedding!"

Wendy continued packing, determined to maintain her composure. "You told me to!"

"Well, I didn't think you'd actually do it!"

"Be careful what you wish for!"

His voice turned accusatory. "So now you're a married woman?"

"Well, it doesn't really count..."

"He said 'I do,' didn't he?"

"Well, yeah, but..."

"And you said 'I do,' didn't you?"

"Yes, but..."

"But nothing! If he said 'I do' and you said 'I do' then he did and you did, 'cause I didn't!"

"Well, if you had said, 'I do' then he wouldn't have had to say 'I do.' But you didn't, so he did!"

They stared at each other across the room, years of love and frustration hanging between them like static electricity.

"So, where does that leave us?"

"I don't know."

"Don't you love me anymore?"

Wendy's hands were steady on her suitcase. "Bruce, I never stopped loving you. This has nothing to do with you... well, wait, I guess it does."

"So now you're married to someone else!"

"That's okay. 'Cause technically, he's married to someone else too."

Bruce's confusion was almost comical. "Let me get this straight -- you married a man who is already married, on top of being gay?"

"I meant he's *practically* married to Kevin."

"Wait a minute. Are gays allowed to marry two people, as long as one is a man and one is a woman?"

"What planet are you on?"

"I really don't know! I'm sorry! I'm a little tipsy right now, and nothing seems to make sense anymore."

Wendy opened her door pointedly. "Look, it's been a long day. I need to get some rest. Let's talk about all this next week when I get back from my honeymoon, okay?"

"Whaa? You're going on *our* honeymoon – with, with *him*?"

Her smile was sugar-sweet and sharp as glass. "Of

course, dear! We wouldn't want to waste Mummy's money now, would we?"

The door closed on Bruce's bewildered face, leaving Wendy alone with her thoughts and half-packed suitcase. She hadn't planned on any of this - the fake wedding, the real friendship, the complicated mess her love life had become. But somehow, watching Bruce storm away from her door felt less like an ending and more like a beginning.

After all, if her gay best friend could commit to being her platonic life partner, maybe there was hope for real love too. Just not tonight. Tonight was for packing bikinis and planning which umbrella drinks to order first in Hawaii. Sometimes the best revenge wasn't living well – it was living exactly as you pleased.

Chapter Nineteen: Paradise Lost (and Found)

The airport buzzed with early morning energy as Mitch and Wendy prepared to depart for Hawaii, looking like the perfect honeymooning couple in their coordinated resort wear. Bob and Kevin had come to see them off, though Bob's dramatic sighs threatened to create their own weather system.

"Boy. I envy you two. Hawaii. The sand, the sun, the men! Oh well," Bob heaved another theatrical sigh, "I guess I'll go scrape the wedding cake off the reception hall ceiling."

Mitch and Wendy exchanged knowing looks. "Bob, if we could take you, we would. But, Wendy's almost mother-in-law only bought two tickets."

The loudspeaker crackled to life: "Flight 407 direct to Honolulu, now boarding."

Bob blew noisily into his handkerchief as goodbyes were exchanged. "Thank you so much, Bob, for making our wedding... so unique," Wendy offered, earning a watery smile.

Mitch pulled Kevin close. "Have fun at work tomorrow. I'll miss you."

"Why is it we always seem to be going on trips away from each other? We need to take a trip together."

"You won't get an argument from me!"

"We'll talk about it when you get back. I'll miss you too."

As Mitch hugged Bob goodbye, he caught a glimpse of a familiar figure ducking behind a ticket counter. But surely Bruce wouldn't be that desperate... would he?

The moment Wendy and Mitch disappeared into the security line, Bob turned to Kevin with manic determination in his eyes. "That's it! I'm going, too!"

"What are you talking about?"

"Come on! Why should they get to have all the fun? We worked hard to make their wedding special, didn't we?"

"Well yeah, but--"

"So why stop now? We can just get tickets for the next available flight out of here, and join in on the fun!" And with that he revealed suitcases he had already packed for the trip.

Kevin laughed at the site. "I don't know, I'm supposed to be at work in the morning."

"Oh, work, smerk! Come on! Now, how much fun can they really have without us there?"

Kevin's resolve crumbled under Bob's enthusiasm. "Oh, alright. I've got plenty of time off accumulated. And you've already packed, so…."

"Great! Now let's fly, cutie pie!"

On the plane, Wendy noticed Mitch's growing tension. "What is it, Mitch?"

He scanned the cabin nervously. "I could be wrong, but I thought I saw Bruce lurking around a ticket counter before we boarded."

"Ha! It wouldn't surprise me. He was a little freaked out last night, so who knows? He's liable to--"

Bruce's head popped up from the seat behind them like a particularly unwelcome jack-in-the-box.

"Holy crap!" Mitch yelped, jumping out of his seat.

"Well, well, well -- what a surprise! Fancy meeting you two here!"

Wendy grabbed Mitch's arm possessively. "Do you mind? We're on our honeymoon!"

The drama reached its crescendo at the Honolulu baggage claim, where Bruce's taunting finally pushed Wendy over the edge.

"So, Wendy, did you bring that sexy red lingerie for your honeymoon?"

She whirled to face him, her patience as extinct as the dodo. "As a matter of fact, I did! And believe me I plan on using it!"

Bruce's jaw dropped. "But I thought Mitch was...?"

"I lied! Okay? You happy? I've been carrying on a secret romance with Mitch for years and now *finally* we can consummate it!"

Mitch's expression matched Bruce's shock as curious travelers gathered to watch the show.

"Mitch, honey, get our luggage! We have a honeymoon to celebrate!"

"Ya know," Bruce offered meekly as Mitch collected their bags, "my Aunt Beatrice gave us that luggage for our wedding..."

Wendy's glare could have melted volcanic rock.

Mitch focused intently on the luggage carousel, determined to stay neutral in this particular lovers' quarrel.

After all, they hadn't even made it to the hotel yet, and already their "honeymoon" had more drama than a soap opera. Somewhere in the San Francisco airport, two more tickets were being purchased for the show.

Paradise was indeed about to get crowded.

Chapter Twenty: The Honeymoon Sweeeet!

"Ready? One, two, THREE!"

The honeymoon suite door burst open to reveal Wendy attempting to carry Mitch across the threshold - a feat that looked significantly more romantic in her imagination than in execution.

Her face turned as red as the "Just Married" sash still draped across her shoulder.

"Wow! Great kick! Did you play soccer?" Mitch inquired from his precarious position in her straining arms.

"Shush! I almost have it."

Mitch responded by examining his nails with theatrical boredom. "Can we hurry this up, please? Oprah will be on any minute."

One tentative step later, physics won out. They collapsed into a heap of laughter just inside the door, forcing an unimpressed bellboy to step over them like particularly inconvenient luggage.

"What can I say?" Mitch offered from the floor. "She's taken this equal rights stuff to the extreme."

The bellboy's expression was unfazed and suggested he'd seen stranger things in this particular suite.

"Mmmmm, whatever. Does that mean she does the tipping?"

"No. That means we don't practice tipping."

"Mitch!" Wendy scrambled to her feet, fishing money from her purse. "Don't mind him!" She leaned closer to the bellboy, stage-whispering, "He's never been with a woman before. It's his first time."

The bellboy's appraising look at Mitch could have melted ice. "You go, girl!" he called to Wendy as he departed.

While Mitch unpacked his meticulously folded resort wear, Wendy explored their suite, Paying particular attention to the enormous jacuzzi tub.

"So my little blushing bride, what would you like to do on our first honeymoon night?"

Wendy emerged from the bathroom with a dreamy expression. "Mmmmm... I'd love to take a nice long jacuzzi..."

"Check."

"Followed by some champagne and strawberries..."

"Check, check."

"And then long passionate lovemaking."

"Uh...check please!" Mitch's voice jumped an octave. "Wendy, you weren't serious about that whole lingerie thing, right? I mean, I... ha, ha... you're such a kidder. Right? Right? Wendy? Hellooo?"

Her shocked expression matched his panic. "Oh Mitch! Of course I was kidding! No offense..."

"None taken. Believe you me."

"I was ready to just invite Bruce to join us if..."

Mitch's eyebrows performed an impressive acrobatic routine.

"Not like that! You know what I mean!"

"Well, why didn't you?"

"You saw him! Acting so pompous and all! I decided to give him a taste of his own medicine!"

"Fair enough!"

"Yeah. That's what I thought. But no matter. When we see him tomorrow I'll explain everything."

"How do you know we'll see him tomorrow?"

"Come on, Mitch! He followed us to Hawaii! I think he'll hang around a day or two."

"Duly noted."

A mischievous glint appeared in Wendy's eye. "So, are you up for my plans this evening or not?"

Mitch clutched his non-existent pearls in mock terror. "I'll go all the way to the point of strawberries, but no further."

"Deal!"

As they settled into their first night as pretend newlyweds, it never occurred to them that Bruce wasn't the only one who might show up tomorrow. After all, what was a fake honeymoon without a few unexpected guests? At least they had the jacuzzi tub and champagne and strawberries to fortify them for whatever chaos awaited.

Besides, Mitch thought as he arranged his evening skincare products on the marble counter, if anyone else crashed their honeymoon, they'd better bring their own bath bombs.

He hadn't packed enough to share.

Chapter Twenty-One: Paradise Interruptus

The hotel lobby sparkled with Hawaiian luxury as Kevin and Bob attempted to check in, though Bob was more interested in sparkling at the bellboy than handling logistics.

"Why don't I ring the newlyweds' suite while you take our bags up to the room?" Kevin suggested.

"What?"

Kevin leaned closer, lowering his voice. "I'll dial their room real slow."

Bob's face lit up like a Christmas tree. "Oh? Okay!" He turned to the bellboy with a dazzling smile. "Follow me, my little boy for bell."

As Bob sashayed toward the elevator with their eagerly attentive escort, Kevin headed for the house phone. His call to the honeymoon suite went unanswered, probably drowned out by the sound of running water and familiar laughter.

Somewhere in that massive jacuzzi tub, his boyfriend was having a perfectly platonic bubble bath with his new "wife."

The hotel bar beckoned like a neon oasis.

"Draft beer, please," Kevin told the bartender, settling in to watch whatever game was playing on the overhead TV.

He'd barely taken his first sip when a familiar voice shattered his anonymous peace.

Kevin? Kevin Johnson?"

Bruce's appearance was about as welcome as a shark at a pool party, but Kevin managed to keep his voice steady.

"Oh, hi Bruce."

The enthusiastic frat-boy hug that followed threatened to knock him off his barstool. "Oh hi Bruce?' Is that all I get? What are you doing here, man?"

"Oh, just having a drink."

"No, I mean, here -- in Hawaii?"

"Oh, is this Hawaii? Those darn buses always drop me off at the wrong stop!"

Bruce's laugh was genuine as he playfully punched Kevin's arm and ordered them both fresh beers. "You didn't mention you were going on vacation."

Kevin's mind raced for cover. "Well, it's kinda embarrassing really. I, uh, sort of followed my girlfriend, Angelina, here..."

"Well, where is she? I'd love to meet her."

"She, uh, doesn't know I'm here yet."

"You mean, she doesn't know you followed her here?"

Bruce's face lit with understanding as Kevin shook his head. The bartender delivered Bruce's beers, and he attacked his with enthusiasm.

"What a coincidence. That's how I ended up here, too. But I didn't think it through. It turns out this hotel is all booked up until morning!"

"So what's your plan? You gonna spend the whole night in the bar?" Smooth Kevin.

Bruce shrugged with the philosophical acceptance of the truly tipsy. "I might pass out on the beach. It's nice and warm outside."

He continued, "Wendy went through with our wedding with another guy!"

"What? She went ahead and married another guy?"

"You were right, dude. I should have listened to you."

Kevin nodded, guilt churning in his stomach like bad mai tais. Here he was, sharing beers with the man whose relationship he'd helped destroy, while his boyfriend took a honeymoon bath with said man's ex-fiancée.

Somewhere, the comedy gods were having a field day. He was definitely going to hell for this.

The irony wasn't lost on him that Bruce had followed Wendy to Hawaii just as he'd followed Mitch - though at least Kevin had sprung for a hotel room.

As they sat drinking in companionable silence, Kevin couldn't help but wonder how this would all play out. Would Bruce finally realize what he'd thrown away? Would Wendy forgive him? Would Bob behave himself with the bellboy?

At least one of those questions was answered by a distant squeal and the sound of dropping luggage, followed by Bob's theatrical "Oopsie!"

Kevin ordered another round. Something told him this was going to be a long night.

Chapter Twenty-Two: Room Service

Paradise looked considerably less idyllic in the harsh morning light as Bruce stumbled in from his beach bivouac, looking like he'd lost a fight with a palm tree. The hotel manager's perfectly pressed uniform and bright smile only emphasized Bruce's disheveled state.

"May I help you?"

"Bruce Hollingsworth. I have a reservation."

A few keyboard clicks later, the manager's smile turned apologetic. "I'm afraid your room is not quite ready sir. Check in usually isn't until three." Taking in Bruce's obvious distress, he added kindly, "But I'll send someone up right away to take care of it for you."

"I'd really appreciate that. Thank you."

As Bruce wandered toward the house phone, the manager caught a passing maid. "Gloria. I need you to clean 1102 immediately."

The manager had barely stepped away for his announced 'nature call' when Bruce returned to the desk, now manned by a young clerk.

"Uh, excuse me? I was wondering how long it will be before my room is ready?"

"Do you happen to know the room number, sir?"

"Yes. 1102."

The clerk checked his screen, noting the room's status as 'cleaned'. "It's ready now, sir."

Unfortunately, 'cleaned' proved to be an optimistic designation. When Gloria arrived with her keycard, the door's security chain brought her up short.

"Sorry!" called a female voice from inside. The door opened to reveal an attractive woman in her thirties, wrapped in a hotel bathrobe.

"Can you come back in a few minutes? I guess I shouldn't have done that electronic checkout through the TV until I was actually walking out the door!"

"No problem. I'll come back."

The timing couldn't have been worse. As Bruce approached his supposed sanctuary, Wendy emerged from her suite next door. Their near-collision sent her diving back inside, but her curiosity got the better of her. She waited until Bruce entered his room, then darted forward to catch the door before it closed.

What she found inside was not what she expected. Bruce stood swaying with exhaustion before an unmade bed, while the previous occupant emerged from the bathroom wearing significantly less than her earlier bathrobe.

The resulting chorus of screams could have woken the volcano gods:

"AYEEEEEEEE!"

"AHHHHHHHHH!"

"BRUCE!"

Wendy fled the scene, her exit accompanied by the bathroom door slamming behind the startled guest, leaving Bruce standing alone in the chaos he hadn't even created yet.

The situation would have been funny if it wasn't so perfectly, horribly aligned with their current relationship status.

Once again, Bruce found himself in the wrong place at the wrong time, this time with a half-naked woman he hadn't invited and an ex-fiancée jumping to the worst possible conclusion.

At least this time he had a legitimate explanation. Though somehow, he doubted Wendy would stick around long enough to hear it.

Paradise, it seemed, had a twisted sense of humor.

Chapter Twenty-Three: Divine Intervention

The elderly priest had been looking forward to his mid-morning snack with the kind of anticipation usually reserved for Christmas morning. He'd assembled the perfect array of treats on his tray, humming contentedly as he made his way down the cathedral aisle.

That's when Wendy burst in, tears streaming down her face, and dove into the confessional.

The priest looked longingly at his snacks, then skyward with a resigned sigh. The Lord worked in mysterious ways, particularly when it came to interrupting a much needed snack time.

"Father, forgive me, for I have sinned."

"You don't mind if I eat, do you?"

"Excuse me?"

"I haven't eaten all morning. I'm starving. Please, I promise it won't interfere."

"Uh, okay... I mean, it is your house and all, so..."

"Thank you," he managed around a mouthful of sandwich. "So, tell me my child, what is troubling you?"

"Well, I believe I may have caused my fiancé to stumble."

"Hmmmm... How so?"

"By marrying my husband!"

The priest nearly choked on his snack. "By marrying your...? Wait! Didn't you marry your fiancé?"

"No. I married my best friend."

"Oh, that's lovely. One should always marry their best friend."

"But I was supposed to marry my fiancé."

"What's wrong with marrying your best friend?"

"Well, aside from the fact that he's gay, and already has a life partner, nothing I guess."

"Ah, so your fiancé is gay?"

"No, no. My husband is gay. My fiancé is straight."

"I see." (he didn't) The priest set down his sandwich, sensing this might require his full attention.

"So, did you marry him to ummm... change him?"

"No, I married him because my fiancé told me to."

"Does your fiancé know that he's gay?"

"My fiancé isn't gay! My husband is gay!"

"Okay, okay. So… what was the question again?"

"I believe that my marrying Mitch..."

"The gay best friend..."

"Right."

The Priest was so proud of himself, "See, I'm catching on."

"Good. Now, I'm afraid that my marrying Mitch may have caused my fiancé, Bruce, to stumble. It was a joke, you know? I just wanted to go through with the wedding, and when Bruce wouldn't, Mitch said he would, so..."

"The stumbling part... let's get to the stumbling part." He picked up his sandwich with empty high hopes.

"Right. Well, I found him with another woman!"

"I thought you said he was gay?"

"No. My husband's gay! Not my fiancé. Ya know, I thought you were catching on? Maybe you shouldn't be eating while we do this..."

The priest set down his food with a heavy sigh that suggested he was reconsidering his vocation.

"So, what should I do?"

He took a fortifying gulp of milk before delivering his verdict. "Go to him."

"Who? Which one?"

"Your gay husband. Your straight fiancé. Your second cousin's lover! I don't care! Just go! Go to one of them. Go to both of them! Go to none of them, but please, I beg you -- just go! Oh, and you are forgiven! Say ten Hail Mary's and five Our Fathers. Now Go! Go! Run like the wind!"

As Wendy left the confessional in a daze, the priest returned to his interrupted snack, making a mental note to suggest that the seminary add a course in modern relationship dynamics. Clearly, the traditional marriage counseling training wasn't covering all the bases anymore. At least the sandwich was good.

Though he had a feeling he'd need something stronger than milk to process this particular confession.

Chapter Twenty-Four: Deep Waters

The jacuzzi bubbles provided convenient cover for Kevin's nervous energy as he found himself sharing yet another intimate moment with his boyfriend's fake wife's real fiancé.

"Wow! Poor Wendy! And you haven't been able to reach her since?"

Bruce shook his head, looking miserable. "Her cell is off. I tried knocking on her door. No answer. She could be out with her *husband*, I guess."

The word 'husband' carried enough bitterness to flavor the entire jacuzzi. Kevin couldn't help but defend Mitch, even if he couldn't explain why.

"Now, wait a minute, why are you getting down on this guy? It seems to me that he was just trying to help Wendy salvage a little bit of herself after you ditched her."

"I didn't 'ditch' her!"

"Then what do you call it? Six days before your wedding you bail on her? I'd say that qualifies as ditching..."

"Hey!" Bruce splashed water in his agitation. "You're the one who told me it was wrong to participate in a marriage ceremony I didn't believe in."

"I don't think I ever used the word 'wrong'..." Kevin backpedaled, guilt making the hot water feel even warmer.

"Well, anyway, I told her from day one that I didn't want a wedding. I didn't feel it was necessary. I just wanted us to be together, that's all. I mean, I love her, man, you know?"

"Yeah, I know... man." Kevin took a deep breath, aware of the irony in what he was about to say. "But uh, if you really want to spend the rest of your life with someone, doesn't that include some compromises along the way? She wants a big wedding? So what? Let her have it! Women love to plan stuff like that."

"Yeah, but what's the big deal? I mean, if we love each other, we love each other, right? We don't need a wedding to prove it."

Kevin thought about all the compromises in his own relationship - his closeted career, Mitch's understanding, and now this elaborate charade they were all caught up in. "It's not about proving anything. It's about doing what's important for one another. Making sacrifices even when it's something you really don't particularly want to do."

Steam rose between them as Kevin continued, speaking from a place of unexpected wisdom.

"Sure, a wedding seems trivial to you, but it's not trivial to her. Sometimes you need to put your petty demands aside and let the woman you love bask in something that gives her great pleasure and joy. Think about this: Do you really want to spend the rest of your life living with a woman who resents the fact that you wouldn't let her have her dream wedding when she had the chance? Or worse yet, do you think Wendy will want to stay with a man who wouldn't support her in one of her greatest dreams?"

Bruce's expression suggested someone had just explained the meaning of life. "Wow! Now, see, if she had explained it like that I would have understood, and would probably have gone through with it in the first place."

"The important thing to remember is that it's all about give and take. You give a little, she'll give a little. That's what life is all about, that's why it's called 'sharing' your lives with each other."

Bruce's smile was one of genuine enlightenment, but Kevin's triumph was bittersweet. Here he was, giving relationship advice about compromise and honesty while literally sitting in a hot tub of lies. He was thinking that somewhere nearby, his boyfriend was probably having a similar conversation with Wendy about Bruce.

The only difference was that Mitch's advice wouldn't involve quite so much personal guilt. Then again, Mitch hadn't spent two weeks convincing Bruce to abandon his wedding. At this rate, Kevin was going to need a much bigger jacuzzi to hold all his karma.

Chapter Twenty-Five:
Truth and Consequences, Part Deux

"Hey! Where have you been?" Mitch's cheerful greeting, complete with freshly towel-dried hair, only highlighted Wendy's emotional exhaustion.

"Hanging out in a confessional."

"Come again?"

She collapsed onto the sofa, massaging her temples. "Oh, Mitch, I think I really blew it this time."

He settled beside her, starting a shoulder rub that spoke of years of friendship. "Now come on, honey... you can tell me anything. I am, after all, your husband. Sort of."

"I caught Bruce with another woman!"

"Are you sure it wasn't Bob? He and Kevin snuck here to surprise us. Isn't that a hoot?"

Wendy bolted upright. "I'm serious, Mitch!"

"Okay, I'm sorry. Tell me everything that happened."

"I snuck into Bruce's suite to surprise him, and lo and behold, a half-naked woman walked out of the bathroom!"

"And what was his explanation?"

"I, I… don't know. I just ran out of there and went into the first church I could find to repent for driving him into her arms." The tears started flowing. "What have I done, Mitch? This whole thing definitely backfired on me. What am I going to do now? Everything's ruined!"

"Seriously?! Come on! You don't know that. You never even spoke to Bruce, right?"

She shook her head sadly against his chest with a sniffle.

"You see? You don't know what really happened. Come on, give the guy some credit, will ya? I mean he did follow you all the way to Hawaii. And you and I both know he loves you more than life itself."

Wendy wiped her eyes, hope creeping back in. "You're right. I guess I really should give him the benefit of the doubt. I mean I at least owe him that."

"Absolutely!"

Grabbing her purse, she headed for the door. "Alright! It's time to face the music. Will you come with me for moral support?"

"I'll walk you in, and then I'm leaving, okay?"

"Deal. And..." She hugged him tightly. "...thanks."

Their confidence lasted exactly as long as it took Bruce to open his door in his robe, revealing Kevin emerging from the bathroom in similar attire.

"AHHHHHHHHH!"

"Kevin?!!!"

Bob's perfectly timed entrance, resplendent in a moomoo and clutching a mai tai, completed the chaos. "I knew I'd find you guys eventually. Always the life of the party. Nice robe, Kevin."

Bruce's shock manifested in stuttering. "You, you know him?"

"Uh, yeah," Kevin admitted.

To Wendy and Mitch. "You guys didn't think that Kevin and I were...?"

Bob laughed. "Oh, honey, we weren't worried. You're not his type!"

"Wait! How do you know him?"

Kevin grabbed Mitch in desperation. "Bruce, there's something I haven't told you yet. This... is my girlfriend, Angelina!"

Bruce's confusion reached new heights. "Huh? But he's a, a, guy, man!"

"God, I hope so!" Mitch couldn't help himself.

"So, Kevin, you're..."

"Gay. Yes. And this is my lover, Mitch."

"Who married, my, my..."

"Your fiancé, yes," Wendy finished. "Only, we were never really married."

"But, rice, I saw them throw the rice!"

"Actually, we used rainbow sprinkles," Bob helpfully supplied. "They're so much prettier, don't you think? And much tastier too!"

Wendy guided Bruce to the nearest sofa before his legs gave out. "Honey, maybe you should sit down." Then to Kevin, "And *you*! We'll talk later about how you know Bruce."

Kevin saluted her with a shaky hand. "Absolutely."

"So, you really didn't get married?"

"How on earth could I really marry anyone but you? You're the one I love with my entire being. Ever since that day you knocked over my hot dogs and sodas at that baseball game and insisted on buying new ones and delivering them to me and my then boyfriend, Lenny."

"Lenny? I remember him. What a sweet guy." Wendy's glare could have melted steel. "I knew that day that I wanted to spend the rest of my life with you, and that has never changed."

Bruce's composure slowly returned. "That's good to hear, because I've been doing a lot of thinking, and I wanna go through with the wedding."

"Little late for that now isn't it sweetheart?"

Bob's commentary earned a chorus of "BOB!" from everyone else.

"I don't think my Dad can afford a whole other wedding..."

"Do you need another big wedding? If you do, then we'll make it happen. But I was thinking we could get married here -- today. That way the rest of our honeymoon can really be... *our* honeymoon!" He glared at Mitch who happily threw his hands up in agreement.

Wendy's smile lit up the room. "That sounds perfect."

"Now about that naked girl..."

"Her name is Patricia. She and I had a good laugh after hotel security finished with me. It turns out she had checked out of this room but hadn't left yet. I don't think she'll be doing that again anytime soon -- we scared her half to death."

"And how about my man?" Mitch joked with a raised an eyebrow at Kevin. "You want to tell me why he's in your suite in a bathrobe?"

"We soaked in the jacuzzi. Just a couple of buddies talking about how impossible it is to understand women."

Their laughter filled the room, washing away the tension of misunderstandings and missed connections. Sometimes the path to true love required a few detours through confusion, rainbow sprinkles, and the occasional jacuzzi heart-to-heart.

At least this time, everyone was wearing robes.

Chapter 26: And Hubby Makes Three

The cathedral's grandeur seemed perfectly scaled for this intimate moment. No elaborate decorations, no Chippendale ushers, no drag queen Supremes - just two couples, one priest who was quite familiar with the whole situation, and Bob clutching his container of rainbow sprinkles like it held liquid gold.

"And do you Mitchell Conrad Pratt take Kevin Thomas Johnson to be your lawfully wedded husband? To have and to hold, for richer, for poorer, in sickness and in health 'til death do you part?"

"I..." Mitch began, then paused, a dreamy smile crossing his face. He broke the fourth wall with a conspiratorial wink to a nonexistent audience. "Hey! A girl can dream, can't she?"

His playful flutter of eyelashes captured everything - the joy, the hope, the acknowledgment that sometimes dreams take different shapes than we expect.

Turning back to the priest, his "I do!" rang with certainty.

As both couples sealed their commitments with passionate kisses, Bob's rainbow sprinkles rained down like tiny pieces of paradise. Maybe it wasn't exactly the wedding any of them had planned, but it was perfect in its own way. After all, love - like life - rarely follows the expected script.

And sometimes the best endings are the ones you never saw coming.

EPILOGUE

The Real Honeymoon

The Hawaiian sunset painted the sky in shades of orange and pink as Bruce and Wendy walked hand in hand along the beach. No unexpected guests, no misunderstandings, no rainbow sprinkles in sight - just two people finally getting their fairy tale right.

"You know what I don't miss?" Wendy asked, letting the warm water lap at her feet.

"What's that?"

"Checking around corners for men and other women in bathrobes."

Bruce laughed, pulling her close. "I promise, the only man in a bathrobe you'll ever find in our room is me."

"Is that a threat or a promise?"

Their kiss was interrupted by a beach volleyball landing nearby. For a moment, they tensed, waiting for Bob to appear in a coconut bikini or Mitch to emerge from behind a palm tree. But it was just regular tourists, apologizing as they retrieved their ball.

Later that night, curled up on their balcony with a bottle of champagne, Wendy sighed contentedly. "This is exactly how I imagined our honeymoon."

"Better than your first one?"

"Well, the company's definitely improved." She grinned. "Though I do kind of miss the Chippendale ushers."

"I can always take bartending classes," Bruce offered magnanimously.

"Keep your day job, honey. And your shirt on."

As the stars emerged above them, they toasted to new beginnings, proper endings, and the blessed absence of unexpected bathroom encounters.

Out and Up

Kevin straightened his tie, took a deep breath, and walked into the partners' meeting. The quarterly earnings report was on the agenda, followed by partnership nominations, followed by his carefully prepared speech.

"And in conclusion," he found himself saying thirty minutes later, "I'd like to thank the firm for considering me for partner. I'd also like to introduce you to *my* partner of five years, Mitch."

The silence that followed felt eternal. Then old Mr. Burlingham, who hadn't said a word in meetings since 1987, cleared his throat.

"Does this Mitch fellow do windows? Because my wife's been looking for someone since that last company went under."

And just like that, the tension broke. It turned out most of the partners had already figured it out - "Your screensaver is *literally* pictures of you two in matching medieval costumes, Kevin" - and the ones who hadn't figured it out were more concerned about the Anderson account than his personal life.

He made partner six weeks later. His first act was to hire Mitch's window display company "Windows to the Soul" to redo the firm's lobby. The rainbow-themed Christmas display won awards and only mildly scandalized the more conservative clients.

A Knight's Tale

"I still can't believe you got Linda Eder to actually perform," Wendy whispered as she helped Mitch adjust his crown. They'd gone full medieval for the commitment ceremony, transforming a local garden into Camelot complete with horses, knights, and what appeared to be the entire cast of a Renaissance Faire.

"Turns out she loves a good gay wedding," Mitch beamed. "At least as long as they're legal and…"

"Don't you dare finish that sentence," Bob interrupted, resplendent in his self-designed Court Jester outfit. "This is a celebration of love, not legislation."

Kevin appeared at the garden entrance astride a white horse, looking every inch the knight in shining armor (though the armor was actually aluminum foil and craft supplies – the armor weighed a TON!

Linda Eder's voice soared through "Someone Like You," Mitch and Kevin exchanged rings and vows beneath an archway of white roses.

They might not have legal recognition, but they had something better - the love and support of their chosen family, plus some really excellent costumes.

Rainbow Weddings Inc.

Bob's business cards read "Uniquely Yours Wedding Planning - Because Normal is Boring." His first client was a straight couple who wanted their entire wedding party to perform a synchronized swimming routine. By the time he finished with them, they'd added fire-eaters, trapeze artists, and a gospel choir performing Lady Gaga songs.

His specialty became what he called "fusion weddings" - combining traditional elements with whatever made each couple unique. He did Star Wars themed bar mitzvahs, steampunk baptisms, and one memorable funeral where the deceased had requested everyone wear Cher costumes.

"The secret," he told his growing staff, "is that there are no rules except the ones we make up. And glitter. Lots of glitter."

His office became a safe haven for couples whose families didn't understand their vision. He had a special talent for winning over reluctant parents with a combination of charm, wisdom, and strategically timed cocktails.

"Love comes in all colors," his commercials proclaimed. "Why shouldn't weddings?"

Oh, and his new magazine *Gay Weddings* was flying off the newsstands!

Divine Vacation

The priest's travel agent was confused by his very specific requirements: "Somewhere with no confessionals, no rainbow sprinkles, and absolutely no relationship drama."

She sent him to a silent meditation retreat in the mountains. For two blissful weeks, he didn't hear a single confession, wedding march, or explanation of who was gay, straight, or temporarily married to their best friend.

He did, however, meet a lovely, retired nun who shared his appreciation for uninterrupted snacks and simple ceremonies.

They started a consulting business advising clergy on how to handle modern relationship dynamics.

Their first book, "Love, Marriage, and Other Things They Didn't Cover in Seminary," became required reading at progressive divinity schools. The chapter on "What To Do When The Bride Marries Her Gay Best Friend Instead of The Groom" was particularly popular.

He still kept a special place in his heart for Wendy and her complicated wedding party. They'd taught him that love, like faith, sometimes requires a leap into the unknown - preferably with some rainbow sprinkles to light the way.

And they all lived fabulously ever after.

THE END

ABOUT THE AUTHOR

Michael Sean McHale has been a writer ever since he could pick up a pencil or pen and write. He is originally from Woburn, Massachusetts. Son of Ellen Sue Garvey and John Fredrick McHale, he is the oldest of seven children that includes Debra-Ann, John, Richard, Kim Marie, Chris and Ashley. He just discovered his father John on Father's Day of 2020 after a lifetime of searching. His discovery lead to meeting five of the six awesome siblings mentioned above.

He worked on the Stock Market in Mutal Funds in Boston for many years until he was diagnosed with HIV in 1990 and given 7 to 9 years to live at the time. This lead him to delve into stand up comedy using the moniker SHADES (always wearing sunglasses) and to make the move to Los Angeles where he (sort of) joked *"If I'm gonna die, I might as well die somewhere warm."* (fast forward 34 years ☺) When he overcame AIDS (he had 4 T-Cells) in 2011 he was all over the news. Google Miracle Mike and FOX News to see his story.

He created his children's educational company Mysteries By Mike in February 1995 and has trained close to one million children how to become spy kidz while teaching them how to read, write, spell and count. He was a writer on the tv show Power Rangers for a brief time and has published his first children's book DinoDogz recently, a fun adventure about dogs that turn into dinosaurs and save the world. Check it out at www.DinoDogz.com and his company at www.mysteriesbymike.com 50% of the profits from DinoDogz benefit animal and children's charities. Follow him on Instagram @MichaelMcHaleAuthor, @MichaelMcHaleActor and @99DinoDogz

ACKNOWLEDGEMENTS

I want to give a shout out to the incomparable Valorie Hubbard and Scott Cargle from Actors Fast Track for their inspiring revelations that brought about major breakthroughs in my actual 'thought processes' that lead this book being written. If you are an actor or writer and are stuck or want to up your game as an artist, I highly recommend that you check them out at www.ActorsFastTrack.com

I have to give a giant thank you to my former neighbor and friend Kelly Holtzclaw for inspiring me to literally think outside of the box which lead to this book being written. He continues to be a great inspiration and for that I am extremely grateful.

I want to thank screenwriter Stewart Wade (Coffee Date, Such Good People) for helping me maaaaany years ago to punch up a couple of scenes in my original script that I adapted for this book.

Lastly, I have to acknowledge every single LGBTQIA+ person, past, present and future who has fought and continue to fight for our simple mantra of "LOVE IS LOVE IS LOVE."

As a Born Again Christian gay man, this has been my mantra from day one when I finally accepted my homosexuality as a part of who I was after contemplating suicide twice, once as a teenager and again a young man because of the (unwarranted) shame and guilt thrust upon me by certain institutions and people. I am beyond blessed and full of joy to be living my authentic self every single day and I hope this fun campy love story will inspire others to be true to their true authentic selves.

And one *last,* last shout to the creators of RYZE Mushroom coffee. I thought I'd 'try' it, and I can honestly say I haven't had this much energy and focus since before the lockdown in 2020. I am not a coffee drinker, so I add lots of cream and sugar. I highly recommend it.

*Please note, I am not a paid endorser for them at all. I have just never been this excited about a healthy beverage in my life. Check them out at Ryzesuperfoods.com

*And their Overnight Oats? WOW!!!! You're welcome.

RESOURCES FOR THE LGBTQIA+ COMMUNITY

WHEN YOU ARE CURIOUS ABOUT COMING OUT OR LOOKING FOR SUPPORT IN YOUR PROCESS OR IF YOU ARE STRUGGLING WITH WHO GOD BLESSED YOU TO BE

ALWAYS REMEMBER: YOU MATTER!

AND YOU ARE NOT ALONE

- Trevor Project Lifeline: (800) 788-7386
- Trans Lifeline: (877) 565-8860. ...
- SAGE National LGBT Elder Hotline: (877) 360-LGBT (5428)
- Suicide & Crisis Lifeline: TEXT OR CALL 988
- LGBT National Help Center 415-355-0003
- Colors Youth 310-574-2813 Ext. 3366
- Los Angeles LGBT Center 323-993-7400
- National Alliance on Mental Illness (NAMI) LGBTQIA+ 323-294-7814

<u>OTHER BOOKS BY MICHAEL & COMING SOON</u>

Available on Amazon Now

1. DinoDogz: EGGZELLENT ADVENTURE

   www.DinoDogz.com

(Dogs that turn into Dinosaurs and save the world!)

2. Mystery Mike's Original Mystery Party Handbook

   www.mysteriesbymike.com

   (From the Party Planner to the Stars!)

<u>COMING SOON</u>

1. *IMMACULATE DECEPTION*
2. *LENA'S DANCE NOVELLA* (based on the film of the same name www.LenasDance.com
3. *MURDER HIGH MYSTERIES (YA SERIES)*
4. *READY FOR MY CLOSEUP*
5. *KOOKIE CLUBHOUSE KINGDOM*
6. *THE MESSENGERS*
7. *THE QUEERBURGS (webseries on YouTube now)*

***Sign up on our email list to hear about all of Michael's upcoming events and book releases and launch parties. HennesseyHousePublications@gmail.com

*Your information will NEVER be shared…no matter how much chocolate they offer. 😊

KEEP SHINING! AND REMEMBER, YOU MATTER!

THIS PAGE IS LEFT BLANK INTENTIONALY

(PLEASE DON'T ASK ME WHY ☺)